HOME

HOME

Eleni McKnight

WordCrafts

Published by WordCrafts Press
Buffalo, Wyoming 82834
www.wordcrafts.net

CONTENTS

For Bryan Sunday-Booth, may your memory be eternal!
I'll see you at the crossroads

CHAPTER 1

A rebel strand of dirty-blonde hair escaped my braid and slipped into my face. I stopped the cart in the chilly hallway and pushed it back into the plait with its companions and pushed the laundry cart into the quarters marked "Maars." This was the doctor's quarters: Ephraim Maars and his goodwife.

They were a strange family; rumors went about the commune about them. They had two sons, one was old enough to be in the militia, and a little girl. Dr. Maars had never taken a second wife, despite being held high in Deacon's esteem, and had never applied for the honor of the Elder's counsel or even the Sub-Elder status.

I had seen the Doctor and his wife on several occasions in the infirmary; she did not walk behind him but beside him, usually talking to him. They were an odd family indeed. Their oldest son, Silas, was a strange boy too; he was awkward and tended to stare too much at people with his giant, dark blue eyes, particularly me. I didn't want Silas looking at me that way, it made me feel funny.

The people in our commune called him *queer*. It was almost springtime, but there was still snow out on the ground and the hallways were always cold. The quarters of the Maars family were warmer than the other quarters I had visited today and there was a strange whirring sound. I touched the wood stove, and it was cool. They hadn't left a fire going. I found the whirring sound: a small metal box that was plugged into the wall. I reached to unplug it, electricity was a luxury in Home. But I stopped short: the doctor got special privileges. I left it alone. Dr. Maars must have left it on for a reason.

As I delivered laundry to the main bedroom for Goody Maars to sort out, I flipped on the light switch. There was a small sink in one corner of the room, and a mirror above it, and I caught a glimpse of my face. I was paler than I remembered, but I saw a smudge of something across my nose. During the wintertime, the water pumps in the Handmaiden House would often freeze, as they had this morning. Vanity was a sin that was looked down upon for the girls of marrying age in this community. We rarely got enough wood to heat the entire cabin, so all the girls like me, who had gotten their cycles, would sleep in a pile on the floor close to the fireplace, which was probably where I had gotten soot on my face. Why hadn't anybody told me I had a dirty face this morning? I turned on the faucet and plugged the sink. Luckily, there was a bar of soap, too. The water filled the basin and a slight rainbow tinge reflected off it as I dunked the soap in to lather.

After scrubbing my face, I examined myself: there weren't many mirrors in Home. Vanity was a sin. But beauty was bestowed by the Great Master on the most virtuous handmaidens to attract a holy husband, according to Deacon. It was difficult to decide if I was vain or just trying to please my future husband, sometimes. I had my mother's watery blue eyes and her nose. My freckles almost masked the pock mark scars from last winter, when I had almost been killed by the swine plague that had devastated the commune. And I had a few other small scars, like the one by my left ear from when I had been running in the courtyard when I was five winters old, and the other one on my forehead, a grim reminder not to run with scissors in school. I still had all my teeth, though; a prize feature. I hoped that one day soon, a good man would ask for my hand in marriage and bring me out of the Handmaiden House. If I didn't get asked to get married by age sixteen, there was the threat I'd be sent to the hard labor camp, where the whores live. The men of our community would go there when their wives are cycling. I don't want to be one of them. Ever. They work harder than those of us in the laundry do and rarely get adequate amounts of food to eat, and are isolated from us. If they hadn't compromised their virginity, they would not be unclean to touch and banned from the main floor of the worship hall. It was their own fault for being so cavalier with their virginity. Deacon impressed upon us that they'd infect the rest of us this way if we weren't vigilant.

I'd love to be the first wife of an Elder; they were the secretaries for their husbands and didn't have to work as hard as the rest of us women in the kitchens and the laundry. They got some luxuries of their choice too, like extra firewood in their quarters. We in the Handmaiden House did not.

I took one last look in the mirror, and gave an approving nod. My skin looked clearer. Pulling the plug to the drain, the green tracking chip light blinked under my skin as my wrist went beneath the water. I dried the last few drops of water from the sink. Hopefully, the Maarses would never know I was here.

Everything was in its place: sorted, stacked with

clean, clear lines. I took a deep breath and smoothed the top article of clothing once more. Perfect. I knew that if left something imperfect, I would be reprimanded. I didn't like the whips. Or the pain that lasted for days afterward.

I could hear the militia training out in the courtyard as I went back into the living room. The soiled clothing meant for me to take back to the laundry was in a pile in the living room, which had a window. I looked out it, to see the militia boys training, and went back to packing the laundry into a sack to separate it. We had a system in the laundry to keep clothing organized so that we didn't wash two different family's sets of clothes together and get them mixed up. The piles already had lights and darks separated, making my job easier.

Beyond the militia, the hard laborer whores were working in the farm fields. I wasn't supposed to look at them too much, but I did so out of boredom, while sorting clothing.

The crops hadn't yielded well last fall. And the whores were to blame. And Deacon said there was a secret sin running through the commune that originated with the womenfolk. I was never told what that sin was, but knew I was partially to blame.

We knew a lot of hunger. But it was better than being out there, alone in the wild, where the reanimated dead and the cannibals lurked. I feared them; I had never seen them but had heard them in the woods.

They were leftover humans from the great flood our Master sent to wipe out the unrighteous of our holy land. There were levels of water stains still on the walls of the commune as proof that the Great Master had wiped humanity this way.

The reanimated dead roamed the woods and ate the

brains of the living. Once bitten, you died, but would come back an unholy thing. The cannibals kidnapped people and cooked their limbs one at a time, to eat. Deacon called them "the Teeth." I have nightmares of them, even today.

I glanced at my buggy and I groaned. I realized I had forgotten a pair of clean socks that needed to be put away. All I needed was Deacon hearing that I was forgetting items; that would risk the whips for sure.

Deacon was our leader and, like the Great Master, he had little patience for poor work. He told us all about the Great Master in his sermons. The Great Master had sent down a book He had written Himself, and trusted all the Deacons in our history to keep it safe. Deacon explained that he often spoke with the Great Master in his office when no one else was around. We had to listen to Deacon, lest we die from another punishment from the Great Master. And if I worked poorly on a consistent basis, that elevated my chances of being sent to the hard labor camp and becoming a whore. I didn't want to be known as poor wife material and age out of the Handmaiden House. I wanted to be loyal to the Great Master and His Son, the Great Warrior and bring more souls into this commune for survival. I ran the clean socks back to the bedroom to set it with the laundry: there was more work to do today.

There was a creak and a footstep. Had someone heard me washing my face when I shouldn't have? I thought the quarters were empty. I hadn't heard anything—Stars, the noise box had blocked out everything! I'd be caught for certain. I held my breath. A door in the hallway opened, and steam poured out. I saw a human form standing naked in the doorway; it was a boy and he was completely… naked.

I stared in horror and shock for a moment. I wasn't supposed to know what boys looked like. His shoulders and chest were strong and muscular and the skin on his stomach was thin and stretched over his muscles. But below that, his hip bones jutted out, leading down to…

His face turned pink, his hand slipping over his bared member and he turned away: he was equally embarrassed and mortified, too.

I turned away, too, Oh Great Master forgive me!

I wasn't supposed to know what boys looked like! Of course, I had seen baby boys naked when it was my turn to bathe my little brothers. I knew women's bodies changed when they got their cycles, but what happened to men when they matured it had always been a mystery to me.

Until now. Now I knew.

I knew.

I knew.

I knew carnal things about men!

My innocence was ruined! This was another reason girls were sent to the Hard Labor camps; knowing too much. And now, I did.

This knowledge was expressly forbidden until Deacon made you a wife to your husband.

The gaze between us was broken.

"I'm - I'm sorry!" I stuttered, closing my eyes, holding up my hand to block my view. "I'm so, so sorry! Please don't turn me in, it was an accident! I swear!"

I stumbled backward out the door, trying to drag my laundry cart out with me.

CHAPTER 2

I ran back to the Handmaiden House, hoping I'd be ignored across the courtyard. I dove onto my bed, taking my blanket and bit into it, screaming.

Why had I disobeyed and used the sink in the Maarses' quarters to wash my face? I knew it was against the rules! I had the explicit directions to leave the clean clothes here and leave, but had not. How did it happen that Silas Maars was in his quarters when he wasn't supposed to be? Why was he in there? He was supposed to be part of the militia, the militia was outside, running drills. I was supposed to be doing my job in the laundry. It had been my fault! I was a sinner. This meant I had carnal knowledge about a boy. Was this enough to sentence me to the Hard Labor Camp? *No, please!* I prayed to the Great Master, mind racing.

Please, please no! I'm not like those girls, I'm a good girl, I want to be good! I know better than to sacrifice my purity for a moment's pleasure. I WANT to be a wife, Great Master! Please, don't give me up to Deacon!

I prayed and prayed, wishing this away, to be forgotten, as if it had never happened for so long, and time got away from me. The door to the Handmaiden House flew open and I jumped at the noise.

"Suzannah?" I heard my best friend Simber come into to the dormitory. Our other best friend, Oakley, was with her. "Suzannah? What are you doing?"

"We were sent to find you," Oakley said. "Come with us. You've got laundry left to deliver and school this afternoon. Remember? We're supposed to skin rabbits in the kitchens."

"And we've got to be there for our families at lunch," Simber added. Her dark eyes narrowed. "We've got so much to do! You're so lazy, sitting here in bed! Come on! Get up!"

"Did something happen?" Oakley asked, concerned. Oakley was gentler than Simber by far.

I bit my lips together and shook my head. Then I nodded.

"What?" Oakley asked, sitting down beside me.

I took a deep breath. "I was only delivering laundry…" I gasped in air again. "I saw something."

"What did you see?" Oakley asked. Like me, her dark blonde hair was falling out of her braid into her eyes, which she tucked away. Then, her eyes focused on mine.

"A boy," I whispered. Oakley tucked my loose strands of hair into my braid again, tenderly.

"So what," Simber snarled. "We see boys everyday in the Common Room and at meals. Everyday."

I wiped my tears. "He was getting out of his shower in his quarters. He was… he wasn't wearing any clothes!" Their jaws dropped and I burst into tears. "Please don't tell anybody!" I begged. "Please! Say you won't!"

"Oh, Stars! We won't," Oakley said, stroking my hair. She hugged me.

"The Great Master doesn't love us once our purity is compromised," Simber whispered. "If Deacon finds out, this is unforgivable. You were doing something wrong, that's why you saw him naked and…"

"It was an accident," Oakley said. "It's not that she… *seduced* him."

"Who was it?" Simber whispered, grabbing my wrist. "Which boy? Matthias? Lucas? Jebediah?"

I took a deep breath. "It was… Silas," I breathed, ashamed, staring at my feet.

"Silas Maars? He's so strange. *Queer*, sometimes. You really saw him?" Simber asked.

"Please don't tell," I begged again. "Please!"

"Come on, we have to go back to the laundry. The Matron knows where we are, we can't dilly-dally all day," Simber said, taking my hand to pull me to my feet. "You've got a mountain of laundry to finish delivering, too."

"I'll help you," Oakley said. "I've got all my work done in the laundry."

"Thank you, Oakley," I whispered.

"You're welcome," Oakley said, taking my other hand. "Don't tell. Promise?"

"Promise," she said. "It's not like you were laying with him. Were you?"

"No!" I cried. "No, never! I'd never… I'd never lay with someone who wasn't my husband!"

"Good," Oakley said as we walked out the door. "It will all be okay."

✛ ✛ ✛

I believe in the Great Master, who sees and knows all.

I believe that He sent his son down from the Heavens and inhabited a human form.

His incarnation was a Warrior, who commanded a flood with his mighty rod.

He smote the unholy with the mighty waters, the virtuous and pure men were taken to heaven; some were returned to help save the weaker sex. Despite the ending of civilization, the great and chosen were still attacked; the unholy rose from their graves and men left to eat their own flesh.

The Mighty Warrior brought what was left of the holy together and gave out His Holy Book: it was entrusted to Deacon. We pledge our allegiance to him and only him until the next coming of the Mighty Warrior who ascended to heaven.

We only hope that we can avoid the reincarnated dead, those that would eat our flesh, and live lives of purity and humility and hard work under Deacon's holy direction.

As it should be.

This was how we began our lessons everyday. The boys study math and science, be in the militia, do carpentry and engineering, but we study animal sciences, child-rearing, food preparation, and laundry and housekeeping. It was because we were the weaker sex that we had to do these more menial chores so we can be better wives.

I assisted with setting the tables and laying out our portion of food for my family for dinner after school. Tonight, the food looked delicious; I wanted to eat some, because most of the rolls were eaten by the men before we had the chance to choose. The rabbit stew had turned out well for early spring. I knew that if the kitchen matron saw me touch my hair like she did today, I'd certainly be caught eating the bread out of turn. I had my job under Deacon; to become the best wife possible. I couldn't afford to do my work poorly. There were fewer and fewer Elders under Deacon these days. Only Elders were allowed to take on second and third wives. Deacon could take on up to a fourth wife if he wanted, though. I only hoped I'd be an Elder's wife. They had the easiest jobs for women and got extra food. I struggled to not hurt from how hungry I was at times.

Once we had the food ready, I brought our rations out to the table. The normal kitchen women enjoyed us being around and doing some work to assist them today, giving them a break from skinning animals and cooking during school. They mostly gossiped and half-heartedly cleaned when the matrons weren't around, watching us instead.

I lined up by the table, my eyes down, as my mother entered with my father. He sat down, and then my brothers. Mother stood beside me, pregnant again. She had had eight pregnancies so far, but the only surviving children were my older brother, my two younger brothers, and me. Losing children and pregnancies were common here, although Deacon had never blamed Goody Maars for any of the children she delivered.

Like one of my younger brothers, I had inherited my father's pale eyes and pale hair, but had my mother's weak chin and huge nose. But I took after Papa. Mother was dark-haired, but it was getting streaked with silver lately, especially at her temples. Papa's hair was cut shorter lately, so short I couldn't tell if he was going gray, yet. I feared going gray: this was the rumor that we all knew that women couldn't conceive any longer. Sometimes, their husbands sent them to be Matrons and took a new, younger and more fertile wife. Sometimes, they didn't replace them at all. I knew Papa was looking for a new wife. Mother was not happy about this.

I glanced up for only a moment to see the Maars boy.

He was looking at me, but looked away quickly, as did I. I blushed and looked down at the broken tiles.

Deacon stood up at the head table, flanked by his sons with his wives and his daughters standing behind him.

"Dear Blessed Master, we have been blessed by You with this bounty and pray to You for a greater harvest this fall. And thank you, Great Master, for giving me the ability to rule over a such a righteous, good community of people and to one day join in your ranks as a Supreme Deity and Ruler in the Stars above. In your name, we pray. As it should be."

My father indicated he was ready to be served. Mother and I stood attentive to him and began to serve him food from the left, then we would serve my brothers. We had been taught this early on when we began helping in the kitchens. We'd clear the dishes from the right, as was instructed, the rules from the Great Master. I kept my eyes to the floor at all times as well. I had been trained this way since I was a small girl. Girls never look men in the eyes without permission. Even wives.

When they were finished, it was our turn to eat. Mother served herself first, then passed the bowl over to me. As I reached for the serving spoon, a hand reached out and snatched my wrist. I whirled around to see one of the Elders looking at me.

"Suzannah Commons, you have disobeyed the Master and compromised your purity."

My heart almost leapt out of my chest. "I'm sorry!" I cried. "I didn't mean to!"

"Heavenly Stars, what did she do?" Mother snarled. "How did you disgrace us this time, Suzannah?"

She hit me over the head and I shrieked, the entire

hall going silent. "Suzannah!" She slapped my ear painfully.

"We will punish the girl," the Elder said. "No need to worry, Mrs. Commons."

"Take her out of my sight," Father said, not looking at me at all. "I have no use for her if she brings disgrace on our family line. I no longer have a daughter."

"Her punishment will be adequate," the Elder promised.

"Please, don't send me to the hard labor camp, please!" I begged and he dragged me away. "Please!"

"Be silent," he snapped, pausing to look at me. He drew back his hand and slapped me across the face so hard that I tasted blood on the inside of my cheek. "We'll see what Deacon has to say."

I choked on my sobs. Everyone was staring at me. I felt my cheeks burn and a dreadful sensation welling up in my stomach. Were they just drawing out my sentencing to the labor camps? If so, it would be a fate worse than death.

CHAPTER 3

Suzannah," Elder Morris said, dragging me to the center of the common room where podium stood, alone. He dragged me, instead to the front of the common room by the pedestal. "Get up," he said. My legs trembled, almost buckling beneath me. He shoved me towards it.

I obeyed.

I hitched up my long skirt to put a foot up on the podium, sobbing, and tried to push myself. Elder Morris shoved me up, and I almost fell off, but caught myself. I found my balance, and bowed my head to hide my tears, although it was useless.

"Keep your eyes to the floor," he muttered. "Deacon has been alerted."

I stood there, staring at the floor, shaking and sobbing. The entire common room was staring at me in my shame, almost greedy. It felt like forever before the doors to the room swung open and Deacon walked in with two other Elders at his side. I tried not to look at them as they paraded in.

Deacon stood in front of me for a very long time. My skin crawled: *What was he planning?* I was so scared, I couldn't stop shaking. *What is he going to do to me?*

Deacon finally circled me a few times, and I could feel his eyes on me. I squeezed my eyes shut, wishing he'd just hurry up already and not draw out the horrible ideas stringing through my head. I felt naked before the whole community.

I shivered, his gaze making me tremble in fear. Was he going to hack my braid off? Strip me of my skirt in front of *every*one? This never happened to girls in Home, but labor whores weren't *girls*. Most of the time, their exile was done in his office, not in the cafeteria or common room. The noise in the room fell to an eerie silence.

"Sons and daughters," he said quietly. The community strained to hear him. "Sons and daughters, look at this poor, deviated child. She is a vessel of sin, as Eve enslaved us to become when she and her sister-wives forced Adam to eat from the tree. She needs guidance and assistance in growing. Unfortunately, her sinfulness got the better of her. Children, sin is a demon we must all fight. Part of the fight is choosing what I command of you when every part of you is insisting on sinning. You must trust me; I have lived in this commune long enough to know and I have the word of the Great Master to carry us along. This poor child was doing her job, the only one The Great Master told me that she's capable of: delivering laundry. One of the young men in the militia fell this morning, and was sent back to his quarters to clean up. She sneaked into quarters, to entertain her own lusts. We must wrestle with lust, to save our souls. She waited with yearning, to see what is forbidden for the pure"

It didn't happen that way! I thought. I dared to lift my eyes. I saw the Maars family at their table. Silas was sitting with his head down, staring at his hands in his lap, his food untouched. The Maars were staring at me. I looked away.

"She saw him naked, a sinful disgrace," Deacon continued. "She's seen more than should be allowed of a pure virgin at a mere fourteen years of life. Ladies, please understand that your only worth, the only thing you have to barter with is your virginity, your purity. If you lose either of those things before I have given you a husband to bed you first, you are ruined for life. You might as well be one of the whores in the hard labor field with your hair cut off and blisters on your hands and sunburns on your faces."

I wished this was over. It felt like it would never end.

"The Elder's Council wants her to be exiled. But, Suzannah's sake, I designate that she is shunned for a day for her sin, disowned by her family."

I knew that trying to plead for leniency was useless; I was already guilty.

"Hopefully, being alone and knowing what it feels like to exiled, even temporarily, she will repent and begin to earn what's left of her purity back. Suzannah, I want you to stand here until we've decided the rest of your punishment. Evening prayers will be delayed until we've decided."

For the rest of the evening, I was stared at and whispered about. I tried to calm my sobs; it wasn't doing me any good. I stood with my hands clasped in front of me, staring at the floor. I could feel their eyes burning me. The children were given free reign in the cafeteria after dinner was finished and the dishes cleaned. The Elders sat at Deacon's table and muttered amongst themselves, watching me. The kids were herded into the cafeteria, and left alone. The children kept their distance, and whispered, staring at me. But, the Elders stood up and ushered them forward. I heard the whispers as they got closer:

"She's as good as a whore."

"Put her out of her misery."

"Unclean."

"Dirty."

"She touched our laundry."

"Slut."

"Impure."

I stared at the floor, trying to wish myself away, to not hear what they were saying about me. Their voices got louder, and I looked up to see the Elders in a ring around the commune's children, closing, pressuring them to converge on me, and their voices began to rise. Some one spit on me and I gasped.

Another one spit on me, then another.

I saw a familiar pair of boots and looked up to see Simber standing there, holding Oakley's hand. Simber glowered and spit. "Merciful stars, Oakley, do it!" she hissed. "Do it, before we get accused of being the same as her!"

Then, Oakley, looking apologetic, took in a deep breath, and then she spat on me, it landing on my skirt. *"Sorry,"* she mouthed at me.

I had never felt so alone or ashamed.

Elder Morris pushed his way through the throng of children back up the podium where I was standing on display. "Your punishment has been decided," he announced. "You will be on a twenty-four hour fast from food and water. You will work your job in the laundry for the full fast. And then, you will be indentured to the Maars family's son for practice for marital housekeeping duties as a wife until you are chosen. Are you ready to start your penance?"

Shaking, I nodded. He did not help me down from the podium.

"Suzannah, understand that you are still a precious daughter to the Master," a voice rang out across the cafeteria. It was Deacon. "This punishment is meant to restore that from your purity that you've destroyed. We are allowing you to stay within the Handmaiden House because the Master still loves you." I dared to glance up to see him standing on the outskirts of the group, behind the Elders. "We all love you so very much."

I nodded, lowering my eyes again.

"This is why I'm giving you a chance to redeem yourself. You, of all girls, should be thankful, now are you?"

I felt Elder Morris's hand strike my back, and I realized he was demanding my agreement. "Yes, sir!" I yelped. "I'm sorry, sir! I'm sorry!"

"Are you thankful?"

"Yes, sir," I whispered.

"It's your sinfulness that can contaminate this entire community! It's the difference between survival and becoming something uncivilized like the Teeth or the Reanimated! If I left you to your own sin and didn't punish you, we'd all be contaminated," Deacon barked. He paused, and the children gave him a path to walk up to my dreaded podium. Deacon's eyes were wild as he grabbed my chin and lifted my face, forcing me to look into his blood-shot eyes. His next words were soft, but not calm. "Now, go. Work hard and do your penance."

A laundry matron took my arm roughly, and pulled me off the podium. I fell to my hands and knees, but she gripped my arm so hard, I fell. I scrambled to get to my feet, lest she drag me.

"If we don't teach this vessel of sin the error of her

ways, how will she ever learn?" the Deacon shouted as I was dragged out. He went on with a homily for the commune about how I sinned. I had no doubts what the sermon would be tonight.

In the laundry, the laundry matron stationed me at the ironing board and gave me a towel to wipe the spit off myself with. I had to heat up the iron on the cast iron stove on my own. I had to be careful to hold the heavy device with a thick cloth so I didn't get burned, and began to iron.

"Pray," the matron snapped. "Pray now!"

I swallowed. *"I believe in the Great Master, who sees and knows all..."*

I finished and she demanded I say it over and over.

The night went on and on.

The public shaming was over, at least. I didn't have to stand in front of everyone any longer. I could do this. I could please the Great Master, apologize for my misdeed, I'd earn back my purity. I was determined to restore what I could.

I prayed until my voice became hoarse and I burned myself from not concentrating on holding the iron. A thick blister grew on my hand, but I kept going, I had to work hard.

"Stop praying aloud," the Matron said. I continued ironing, but burned myself a few more times. "I didn't tell you to stop all together," the Matron snapped when I sucked on my damaged finger for a moment. I continued with my work, despite the oozing blister bubbling under my fingerprint.

Once I had the last of the ironing done, he Matron told me to start mending. Determined, I got out the needle and thread, and began with tiny stitches. Good work meant that the Great Master was with me, and that would show I was forgiven, I was certain of it. I'd be forgiven, I prayed as I concentrated on making straight lines with the rusty sewing machine.

I continued with my punishment. My hands and my arms got tired as I found the torn seams to run under the machine, pumping with my foot, but the blister on my finger made it difficult to thread and re-thread the needle. I couldn't let myself fail: if I did, that meant the Great Master did not forgive me. My back ached from arching over, and my eyes became dry and itchy from concentrating on the needle and keeping it threaded. The Matron glowered at me while she knitted.

"Are you finished, yet?" she sneered.

"No, ma'am," I answered.

"What's left?" she asked, setting the needles down and striding over.

"These pieces can't be mended by machine," I explained.

"Stand up. Don't sit to stitch by hand," she replied.

Hands shaking, I stood up and began sewing, my eyes crossing from trying to thread the needle for hand-stitching, but the blister burst onto the fabric, but at least there was fabric to drain the burn. I gasped.

"Suzannah," the Matron warned, the edges of her mouth curving down.

I squeezed my eyes shut and opened them again to focus better.

The morning light peeked out at dawn, and the girls from the Handmaiden House appeared, having gathered the morning's laundry. They were probably forced to ignore me by Deacon's orders, but I heard the whispers.

Simber and Oakley glanced in my direction and tried to mouth something, but the laundry Matrons rapped them on their backs as a warning.

More mending was tossed into the pile at my feet.

My mouth was so dry by the time the other Handmaidens left for school. All I wanted was some water, and fresh pitchers were brought in, but I was not allowed any. I only hoped I was being forgiven for my sins. I tried to hold out and be strong, despite my blurring vision and the sickness and bile rising in my throat.

"Matron?" I begged.

"Shh!"

The iron tumbled out of my hands to the floor.

"Matron?" I whispered as my knees buckled under me. I crumbled to the floor.

CHAPTER 4

I tried my hardest to pull myself back up. But the hot iron hurtled downwards towards me, singeing through my clothes and burning my forearm that I threw up to protect myself.

"Suzannah?" the Laundry Matron shouted. "Get up now. Now! Off the floor."

I felt her cane strike me across my back.

"Suzannah!" she shouted, as another blow landed on my shoulder. "Suzannah," she snapped. "Get up!"

The darkness claimed me.

It felt like only a moment later, someone picked me up and putting me into a bed. I whimpered.

"It's going to be alright, Suzannah. Just rest," a male voice said. I heard the squeak of wheels: I was on a gurney.

I opened my eyes to see Dr. Maars pushing me down the hallway.

"Rest," he repeated. This wasn't a trick or a test... I hoped. I closed my eyes and he threw a blanket over me.

A cold breeze hit me, then a flash of light: it was a clear day outside, but bitter cold. He pushed the gurney outside. I closed my eyes against the bright sunlight.

"Just a moment, we're almost to the infirmary.

Bear with me," he muttered. The cold wind was tearing into my burnt shoulder like a knife wound. He pulled the meager blanket up over my shoulders.

He pushed me into another building, a warmer one, thankfully not the Handmaiden House. I assumed it was the infirmary: it smelled like medicine.

He picked me up and set down in a bed that didn't roll. The sheets had been warmed up.

"How is she?" a woman asked.

"Dehydrated. Blood sugar is most likely low."

I felt someone lift my upper lip.

"Iron is low, too," she said. "Suzannah, dear, we're going to take care of you, your punishment's over. Let's get her on the NG."

After they put a tube in my nostril and down my throat and put an IV in my arm, they left me to sleep beside the warm radiator.

I dreamed of the horror that awaited me outdoors with the reanimated corpses coming to eat our innards. Their waxy skin, bloodshot eyes. Or the cannibals skinning me alive, rail-thin and hungry, looking at the flesh in my cheeks greedily, making me watch as they sliced off my limbs and my cooked my flesh, then my tongue, to eat. I had no fences to defend myself since I had been kicked out of the commune, I had no militia to defend me. Everyone was inside. They couldn't hear my cries, or maybe they did, they were ignoring me. I was alone, against the elements, everything Deacon had warned us about was happening to me alone because I had sinned. I sinned.

I woke up, clawing and screaming. My arms struck another human form and I opened my eyes.

"Suzannah, you're fine," the woman said to me. She was older, maybe my mother's age. Her eyes were watery-blue and her hair blonde, like mine. I focused on her, and she smiled gently, stroking the hair out of my face. I recognized Dr. Maars' wife. "I stayed to make sure you were alright," she said.

I look around. A few other commune members were resting in beds down from mine. An Elder who we had been told had a heart attack was four beds down from mine, looking grayish.

"Would you like another blanket?" she asked.

I shook my head.

She stroked my hair so gently. It felt so nice to have another person touch me like that. Her fingertips made my back and shoulders relax. The stress leaked out of me, I almost went back to sleep.

"You're allowed to speak to me," she said. "Your punishment's over."

I opened my mouth to tell her thank you for the medical care, but I was interrupted by Dr. Maars.

"Marissa, how is she?" he asked. I saw the doctor coming through the aisles. He was older, very thin, his hair long and in a ponytail, his beard unkempt. The men in our commune usually kept their beards trimmed and neat in the winters, and their hair cut short. Dr. Maars seemed to forget about this.

"She's awake," the woman said. "The burn is still raw on her shoulder. Suzannah, I'm Goodwife Maars. You've been here before?"

I nodded, biting my lip. I saw a needle and tube stuck into the inside of my elbow. I reached to touch the foreign object.

"Don't touch that," she warned.

I pulled my hand away. "I'm sorry."

"It's delicate. We don't want you tearing your vein, it would bruise."

"I did something so horrible," I whispered, thinking about how I had just failed to complete my punishment. "I'll never get forgiveness."

"Suzannah," Dr. Maars said. "Do you *request* forgiveness?"

I nodded.

"I'll let the Elders know."

"But, I'm not forgiven."

"You don't need to request forgiveness from me," he said, and walked away.

"Suzannah, can you get in to this wheelchair?" Goodwife Maars asked. I nodded and carefully pulled the covers back. She carefully and slowly removed the feeding tube from my nose, and the sensation made me sick as it came up from inside my throat to the back of my mouth to my nose. I cried out softly in disgust. "I know this is uncomfortable, dear." I saw the end come out. "This was the only way to feed you." I could see that she was about the same age as Dr. Maars as she moved me into a wheelchair. Most wives were at least twenty years younger than their husbands. Most boys went into the militia and were unsuitable for marital arrangements until they had spent a few years training. That's when they married Handmaidens and started families. There was usually a large age gap between husbands and wives.

She wheeled me down the hall.

"Where are we going?" I whispered.

"I'm taking you to the bathtub," she said. I went rigid hearing this. "Everything's fine. The worst part of your punishment is over." She brought me into the bathroom and started running the water. She flipped on a white noise machine. "How hot do you like it?" she asked.

I shrugged. I hadn't bathed in a while. "I don't know," I admitted.

"You can undress now," she said, getting some towels out of the cabinets and a canning jar.

I stood up and she waited expectantly, holding the towels. I realized she meant for me to undress in front of her. I hesitated.

"I help women birth children, Suzannah, I've seen everything. Nothing will shock me, I promise."

I was being silly: Goody Maars was a girl, and I dressed and undressed in front of the other girls in the Handmaiden's House daily. I undid the ties on the back of my nightgown that I had been dressed in. My underthings had been removed, too. When I was naked, she assisted me into the tub.

"Just relax and put your head down. We need to wash your hair."

I nodded and let her dunk me under the water as she got some of the hair soap out of the canning jar and some delousing solution. The water felt so good, except on the burn on my shoulder near my collarbone. And my finger that was blistered, but my hand was easier to keep out of the water. The water was too hot on those burned parts of my body, but other than that, I enjoyed this feeling. It was so wrong for me to have something so comfortable after the last two or so days.

"You can talk, you know. This is a safe place. I've already told your mother you've been whipped. She shouldn't want to do it to you by now, I hope. But I can't stop her if she does. It's her right… I won't tell anybody anything you say to me. We're going to dress you clean clothes and put you back to bed when you're done here in the bath."

I rubbed my eyes with the heel of my palms, but didn't speak.

She got out a cloth and dipped it into the water and rubbed some of the soap on it. "Silas is my oldest living son. He's a good boy, it's alright, he isn't angry with you. A little embarrassed, maybe, but not angry."

My cheeks burned. How could she be so nice to me when I had sinned so violently against her son?

"These things happen," she continued, rubbing my back and shoulders with the cloth. "Silas was sent home from training early because he got too dirty. He got in a fight with some of the other militia boys, and they shoved him the mud this morning. He was so wet, he started to show signs of hypothermia during drill, and they sent him to the infirmary, and I sent him back to our quarters for a hot shower. It wasn't planned. He wasn't scheduled to be there, dear."

I gulped back a sob.

"You couldn't have known. I know he'll accept your apology." She started applying the delousing solution to my scalp. "The Elders have their rules. I don't think what you did was a sin; it wasn't on purpose. What you saw wasn't a bad thing. You're not a bad person for seeing something accidentally."

"But I still think about it," I finally admitted. "That's a sin."

I heard her chuckle softly. "No, you're just curious," she said. "You're a good girl, Suzannah, I can tell. Curiosity isn't a sin. To be curious about the opposite sex is natural for girls at your age. It's natural for boys to be curious about you, too. I was like that when I was your age. Most girls are, but are too afraid to admit it."

I began to panic: was her son going to be allowed to see me naked?

Are they going to strip me naked and send me to the hard labor camp?

"Suzannah, calm down," she said gently, squeezing my good shoulder. "A few deep breaths?" I did as she asked, and she picked up a comb and began combing out my wet hair. "The punishment is in the past. What you saw, how you keep remembering it, it's normal. You're going through puberty. This is the period of time when your body stops being a child's and becomes a woman's who can make babies and feed them and… many wonderful things are happening. It started with your menses and will continue until you're too old to have children. You are a wonderful, sacred, important thing, do you understand that? We are what creates life. Mankind couldn't continue without us. Being born a girl doesn't make you unholy or less intelligent, dear."

"We're vessels of sin," I whispered. "We make the men do things without even realizing it. We're bad for that alone."

"No, we're not," she said softly. "There is a secret in this commune, and I want you to know it. It can be a very dangerous one to know, too: good people sometimes make mistakes. That's doesn't make you a bad person. You are just as holy and good and important as the most important man in this commune. We all are. We're part of a wonderful and mysterious part of the circle of life. The Master made us that way, because He loves us, no matter what Deacon says." She continued to brush my hair and then braided the wet locks. "My dear, you are welcome to come here and ask me questions any time. This room and my husband's office are safe rooms when it's just you and me in it. Understand?"

I shook my head. "The Master hears everything," I whispered.

"I know. But the Master isn't as terrible as the Elders and Deacon say He is."

"But Deacon reads from the holy book," I whispered.

"I've seen and read the holy book that Deacon refers to when he lectures us," she replied. "You're safe when it's just you and me." She smiled. "Trust me."

I blinked back tears. Why would she tell me this? To get me into more trouble? Of course, what she said went against Deacon incredibly. I could get her into trouble if I wanted, but I'd be in trouble too, for listening to her talk like this. I decided it was best to trust her and keep this conversation a secret. "Alright. I will."

Once she was done braiding my hair, she allowed me to sit in the bathtub for a while by myself, giving me another handful of soap to wash the rest of myself. When she returned with freshly folded towels, she helped me out of the tub, she patted me dry with a towel and dressed me in a fresh tunic and skirt. She treated my burn with the sap from a plant— an aloe plant, one she specially grew in the plant nursery. It felt cool and refreshing on my aching burn, and she bandaged it up to keep it clean. "This should clear it up in a few days," she said.

She wheeled me back up to the bed where Elder Morris, who had chastised me, was waiting… with Silas, his eyes to the floor, his face turning red. I felt my heart leaping out of my chest. I barely remembered to cast my eyes to the floor in time.

"You served your punishment," the Elder said. "Are you ready to repent? Suzannah, can you hear me?"

The lump in my throat was growing. If I spoke, I'd cry. But I had to. "Yes, Elder Morris," I choked out, the reluctant tears welling up in my eyes.

"Stand up. Are you ready to ask forgiveness from Silas?"

My knees shaking, I stood. "Y-y-yes, Elder," I stuttered. I thought my knees would buckle.

"Look up, dear," he said softly.

I looked at Silas. My vision was still blurry.

Silas, with his clothes on, was a little different than I remembered. His eyes were green with flecks of brown in them. He had thick, pillowy lips, and the scruff of a beard growing over the few pox scars he had, I could see his hair had been shorn short for the militia. I could focus on his face, more, now. He looked a little beaten-up; he had a black eye and his lower lip was a little swollen. There was a trickle of sweat going down his temple and his face was still red. Despite it all, I felt a fascination. I had never really looked into Silas's face and seen how perfectly proportioned it was. I wondered if it was symmetrical without all the bruises and swelling.

I realized I wasn't breathing. "Silas…" I began, taking a deep breath. My cheeks burned with embarrassment. "I'm sorry I saw you naked. Will you forgive me?"

I saw his face was turning red, too. "I forgive you," he said. "It was a mistake."

I glanced up. How odd that he used that word. I saw Elder Morris's nostrils flare and his eyes narrow. After a long, uncomfortable silence, Elder Morris spoke. "As it should be. All is forgiven. Suzannah, you are to practice your housekeeping and cooking skills as a wife on Silas. You are to wake up early everyday to make whatever Silas wants for breakfast. You will do this for every meal. Every night, you are required to go to the Maars's quarters to clean for him, unless you fall ill. You are to do your required work in the laundry as well as Silas's."

"Will I be allowed to go to school?" I asked.

The Elder shook his head. "You are finished with school, Suzannah. You will not have time for it any longer."

I nodded, although I knew not to argue. "Am I to be Silas's wife?"

Elder Morris chuckled, and I blushed. Was I being stupid? I couldn't tell. "No. We have other plans for you, but you must keep in mind; you damaged your purity with your actions, you are worthless right now in the eyes of the Great Master. Sex and deviant, carnal thoughts before marriage are worse than murder for a woman. The loss of virginity means you have turned completely from the Master."

"Am I still a virgin?" I interrupted, completely by accident.

"Yes, you are," Goodwife answered suddenly. She hadn't left my side. "The veil is still intact." The Elder glared at her. "My husband examined her and said so."

"You should see to your wife," he snapped at Dr. Maars, who was standing by, tending to another patient in the infirmary. I got the feeling the Doctor and Goody had been eavesdropping the entire time. The Elder stopped for a moment to glare at Goodwife, and then turned back to study me. "Your willingness to serve Silas will help redeem you and make you suitable material to serve your future husband. You are making a better woman of yourself and I am proud of you. Deacon is, as well. I'm going to leave now. As it should be." He kissed me on the forehead. "Silas?"

He and Silas walked out together, he lectured Silas on the importance of concentrating in the drills and always being on guard.

"Rest some more," Goodwife Maars told me, indicating the bed. She smoothed the sheets and blankets nervously. She glanced in at the exit of the infirmary that Silas and Elder Morris had just disappeared through, brow furrowing. She fluffed my pillow. "You'll need it."

CHAPTER 5

Once Dr. Maars released me from the infirmary, I walked across the snow-crunchy grounds to the Handmaiden House. The girls were all getting to bed at this hour. I crossed the suspicious glances and whispers to my bed, to pick up my blanket and I changed into my nightdress.

After changing clothes, I went over to the lone fireplace, which had a small, pitiful fire in it. Some of the boys in the militia had offered to cut more wood for us to keep the girls in the Handmaiden House warm, but Deacon denied the request. He insisted they train instead and we'd make do with what we had. Deacon got reports that the Teeth were close by, the militia had to be ready for them.

I put on socks and went to where Simber and Oakley were waiting. Simber backed off.

"Suzannah! What happened in the infirmary?" Oakley asked, her face concerned, rushing towards me.

I decided to not tell her the strange things Goodwife Maars told me. "They put me on a tube to feed me," I admitted.

I decided to keep Goodwife's words to me a secret. "I got a bath."

"You were supposed to be punished," Simber hissed. "You were bathed?"

"The water was cold," I lied. Goody had been too nice to me; I should not have confessed the bath. "I'm going to start making his meals, cleaning his quarters, and doing his laundry, too. They say it's going to assist me in getting me ready to serve a husband."

"That's a good thing," Oakley said. "I was afraid they'd sentence you to the hard labor camps. And make you…"

"A hard labor whore? I know," I whispered, resting my chin on my knees.

"You'll have to be careful," Oakley warned. "They don't need as many wives these days. There're fewer and fewer men to marry. More of us will be sent to the camps, soon." Two girls, Colleen and Katlyn, had just aged out and didn't marry. It was devastating when they reached their 17th winter and disappeared from the Handmaiden House.

"What about the boys in the militia?" I asked, thinking of Silas. Even if he had told the Elders about me, looking into his face to apologize… I wondered if he was a good man to be a wife to… "Why don't they let them start marrying?"

Oakley and Simber looked at each other and then at me. "They're too young to get married," Simber snapped as if I were stupid. "You got lucky with the punishment for that sin."

"She's right," Oakley said. "I don't want to see you fail. I want us all to be wives to Elders. Wouldn't that be nice?"

I shrugged.

"Could you have been more foolish?" Simber muttered. "Of course you were caught."

"Why did you spit on me?" I asked.

"Suzannah, you're impure now. Maybe not as impure as the hard labor whores, but you're dirty. I can't really be friends with you, do you understand?" Simber said. "I want to get married, too. You'll get sent off to the camps."

"No, she won't!" Oakley cried. "She hasn't been, yet!"

"There's still time," Simber said, turning from me. "She'll go there yet."

"Lights out," the dorm Matron said, flipping off the dim electric lights, leaving us illuminated by the fire. I sat down on the floor near the pile of girls sleeping together, but all the other girls wiggled away from me.

The message was clear: I was dirty. Unclean. Nothing I could think of would ever clean the black spot on me of sin.

And I would not sleep well for a long, long time after tonight.

I was not expecting the dorm Matron to wake me early and make me get dressed. "Suzannah," she hissed, shaking me.

I groaned softly, opening my eyes. It was still dark as pitch out; the sun wasn't anywhere close to rising.

"Go, wash your face and go to the kitchens," she whispered.

I brushed my blanket aside, leaving the girls sleeping in a pile by the dark fireplace, although it was far too early to be awake. I rubbed my eyes and made up my bed.

In the outhouse, I washed myself with a semi-frozen bowl of water before dressing to go to work, although I didn't need it so much. The commune was just waking up and the overnight guards watched me as I cross the courtyard from the guard tower.

Silas hadn't made a specific request for breakfast, so I assisted with the food preparation with the rest of the cooks and assisted with getting the Maars's table ready for breakfast. I wondered if he'd give me an order for lunch, hopefully, it was something we had in the smokehouse or the food stocks.

Since Goody Maars was oftentimes called away for infirmary reasons, and she rarely was able to prepare her own family's table. The other wives took turns making their meals for them. But now, it was up to me. Goody Maars arrived, holding her little daughter's hand, and stood next to me.

The little one grinned up at me with gap teeth. "Hi," she whispered. "I'm Tellulah. I'm Silas and Noah's little sister. They call me Telly."

"Hi," I replied.

"What's your name?" she whispered.

"Suzannah," I whispered back.

Goodwife Maars smiled and stroked Telly's hair. "Shh," she whispered. I realized the smile was extending to her eyes, although she was trying not to smile.

Telly me gave me another giant grin.

We weren't supposed to talk, but I grinned back- she was a cute little girl. She seemed to like me, despite my damaged reputation. It felt good to smile, again.

Dr. Maars, Silas, and a boy I assumed was Noah, sat down at their table. When Deacon arrived, he said the breakfast prayer and we were allowed to serve the men. Goodwife Maars began to serve the Doctor, and I noticed that as she put more food onto his plate, he put a hand on her wrist.

"Stop," he whispered. "That's enough."

"You need to eat, dear," she whispered, pulling her wrist out from under his hand to put another scoop of protein mush into his bowl. "You have an important job."

"So do you. So does Telly," I heard him reply. I saw him squeeze her wrist and she put the spoon back into the protein mush and handed the bowl to me.

I scooped a spoonful into Silas's bowl. I only had one spoonful in before Silas said, "That's plenty."

"My turn!" Telly cried, too loudly. Telly was known for being too loud, the Elders frequently shushed her with a swat to the rear. I handed her the bowl. She very carefully put a spoonful into Noah's bowl and then another with her mother's supervision.

"That's too mu-uch!" Noah cried.

"That's all he needs for now," Goodwife Maars said to her daughter. "Good girl."

The men in the family began to eat.

We had to wait until they were mostly done before Dr. Maars invited us to sit down and eat.

They talked about strange things; Silas's training, Noah's school work. I found this strange. My life was never talked about unless I was doing poorly. Papa would question us, but if he already knew, that was the worst. That meant we were in trouble. But Dr. Maars already knew his children's accomplishments and beamed.

I felt an unsettling twinge of jealousy. He turned to me, asking me what my day could contain, and I bowed my head.

"I have work, then cooking, sir."

"And after that?"

"Dinner, worship, and cleaning for Silas."

"Good, good."

"Papa, when are we going to the Ruins?" Telly asked.

"Shh," Goody shushed.

"I have drills today," Silas piped up. "We already starting training early this morning, and I'll be back at ten if you need help in the infirmary."

The Ruins. But that was all it was; a mention. I had heard of the Ruins before, but we were told it was too dangerous to go out that way, what with the reanimated dead roaming the forest.

We hadn't seen the reanimated in a long time, though. But the Teeth were threatening to make an appearance if Deacon knew correctly. What was the big deal about the Ruins anyway?

It felt strange to eat at the same time that the men in the family were eating. I personally had never had more than two scoops of protein mush at breakfast before. Telly squirmed and wiggled beside me as she ate.

"We're going to learn numbers today," Telly whispered loudly to me. "I'm so excited!"

"Remember to use your indoor voice, Telly," Goodwife Maars reminded her. "Is anybody else hungry for more?"

I kept my head down. The men came first.

"Mama, can I have more?" Telly asked.

"Yes, you may. Suzannah, don't be shy," Goody Maars said.

I looked up in shock: I had never been offered second helpings before.

"I'm full," I lied.

"Are you sure?"

I thought for a moment, but then I nodded. I wondered if this was a test from the Elders. I didn't want to fail it. Surprisingly, Goody Maars put another spoonful of the mush into my bowl. "Eat anyway," she commanded. "You don't want to lose your strength."

I did as I was told.

"May I ask a question of Silas?" I asked, keeping my gaze into my bowl.

"Yes, go ahead," Silas said.

"What do you want to eat for lunch?"

He didn't answer. I looked up to make sure he was alright, and he was looking straight at my face and he offered me a shy smile. A friendly smile, as if to reassure me. My cheeks burned. "Whatever everybody else is eating."

The warning bell rang. I assisted Telly and Goody Maars with taking the dishes to the kitchens before going on to the laundry.

Upon arrival at the laundry, I was informed I was no longer allowed to deliver laundry to the quarters due to my bad behavior. I now had to iron and fold all the clothing in regulation style, which made me a little bit light-headed from the iron's steam.

An hour before lunch, I was told I needed to go to the kitchens to cook for Silas and was excused with the promise I'd finish my laundry quota this afternoon while all my other friends were in school.

At lunch, Dr. Maars stopped Goody Maars from putting too much food on his plate, again. He limited how much the boys got to eat before we had a chance, and then distracted me by asking me how my morning in the laundry went.

"It went well," I said. "I'm going to be allowed to finish my laundry quota this afternoon."

"Shouldn't you be in school like the rest?" he asked.

"No, sir. I'm done with school," I answered, looking up, surprised. Hadn't he known?

A heard the wooden spoon tap the side of my bowl,

and I saw Goody had put more mush in. "Eat," she commanded.

I thought this strange; men usually ate a majority of the food, women got what was leftover. I was afraid to eat it; I was so afraid that this was a test of me. I reluctantly ate my portion.

"Silas?" I asked as we had begun to gather the dirty dishes.

"Yes?"

"What would you like for dinner?" I asked, avoiding his eyes.

All I got was silence. I looked up to see if everything was alright, and he was staring at me. "Whatever everybody else is eating," he said quietly.

In the laundry, I worked to finish my quota with some of the other wives. Afterward, I was sent straight to the kitchens to assist the cooks. I struggled: there were so many pots and pans, and it was up to me to clean them all. I had to get to dinner and then worship, and then to clean Silas's room. I guessed I'd be getting back to the Handmaiden House at a later hour tonight.

Again, the Maarses ate in a strange manner. Again, Silas did not request anything strange or different. Again, Goody put more food on my plate than I asked for. Again, I was puzzled by their odd methods altogether.

When I arrived back in the common room from taking the dirty dishes to the kitchen, the older children in the Commune were gathering. A few were playing games, but most everyone stared and whispered at me as I passed.

"What's it like, being a hard labor whore?" a boy asked.

"Ignore them," Oakley said, taking my arm.

"She's a slut. She's probably lost her virginity already. Oakley, how can you stand touching her? She's dirty," another girl named Angel asked.

"She's not dirty!" she cried, although she had stopped holding onto me.

"Oaks, get away from her," Oakley's older brother warned. "She's filthy!"

I felt something hit the back of my head; it was a small rock. I shrieked in pain.

"Unclean," a girl from the Handmaiden House snarled.

"Unclean!" another one shouted.

"She's unclean! Unclean! Unclean!"

"Dirty," another boy hissed.

"She has leprosy!" another girl sang out.

The mothers were watching, but not doing anything. I was horrified and humiliated. If they did this to me, was there a chance I'd be kicked out of the Handmaiden House? Someone spat on me. Oakley and Simber were pulled away and dragged into the crowd.

I crouched to avoid the blows and the spit, but they just came faster and faster. I couldn't say anything; the Elders were watching. The kids were chanting that I was filthy and had leprosy. I curled into a ball, down to the floor, shaking.

"Stop it!"

I saw Silas push his way through the crowd.

"Leave her alone! She's doing her punishments!" Silas said.

"She's still dirty," a boy from the crowd said.

The other kids laughed, but the assaults did not continue.

I looked up and saw the crowd around me was parting for Silas.

"Suzannah, it's time for us to go to worship," he said, slipping and arm around my shoulders. He grabbed my arm with the other one and brought me to my feet. "I'll escort you there."

Sniffling, I let him lead me out.

"Don't mind them," he said. "And don't put up with them calling you names. You're not a bad person."

"Yes, I am," I whispered.

"Nobody's a bad person. We just do bad things sometimes. And make mistakes." In the foyer of the worship hall, Silas used his jacket to wipe the spit off my hair and the tears from my eyes. "I was there. They weren't. A mistake means you didn't do anything wrong," he whispered.

"Doesn't it embarrass you?" I asked. "That I sinned against you?"

"It was an accident," he said. "If it were a sin, you'd have sneaked in there on purpose and been waiting for me, to see me. You were only doing your job."

I looked back up into those green eyes.

"I think your punishment is completely unnecessary. And wrong."

"Don't speak out against the Elders and Deacon!" I whispered.

"I'm not speaking out against them. This punishment is only designed to break your spirit. You're a good girl, Suzannah. You don't deserve this. Will you let me escort you into the chapel?"

I didn't answer.

"If you don't want me to, I understand…"

"No, I do!" I cried. I wasn't supposed to turn boys down when they offered to do something nice for me. "I… I do. Thank you."

He held out an arm for me on the right, which I took.

It was rare that boys escorted unmarried girls into the chapel, but Silas was treating me like I was something special.

Was I? Was I as good as he and Goody told me I was?

We walked in, and the people already there turned to look at us. I saw shocked and revulsion at my presence. My mother and my siblings were sitting in their pew, and my mother looked furious. "Suzannah, what do you think you're doing?" she snapped.

"She's sitting with my family," Silas answered, taking me to the pew. He slipped an arm around my shoulders and guided me into the Maars family bench to sit. "I'm glad you're here with me."

I wasn't sure how to respond. "I… I…" What did I say? "I um…"

"Hi, Suzannah!" Telly whispered excitedly, tumbling over her father's knees into the pew. She was completely unaware of what had just happened to me. Dr. Maars smirked and patted his daughter's tousled hair as she approached me.

"Not a good time, Telly," Silas whispered.

"Can I sit in your lap?" Telly whispered to me, ignoring him. I was stunned. She took my silence as a yes and climbed into my lap contentedly. I supposed she was alright with all this. I decided I'd be, too. I slipped my arms around her, she was warm and soft. People stared at us in horror.

"I made this for you," Telly whispering, getting something out of her dress' pocket and handed it to me. I opened it, and it was a paper doll with my name written on it in her childish scrawl.

"Thank you," I whispered. "I'll keep it forever."

Telly grinned up at me, excited, her front teeth gapping.

Deacon stood at the pulpit in his robe and stole and waited as everyone filed in. The hard labor whores filled in upstairs, not allowed to sit in the pews, but they had to sit on the floors in the upper balcony. I didn't want to be one of them, worked half to death in the factories and the fields, partially starved, and taking multiple soldiers each night from the militia, their hair shorn to their shoulders. It was so shameful to be one. They all died so young, eager to find out if the Master actually wanted them or not, whereas we, the people sitting in the pews downstairs, were guaranteed.

Once we were all sitting and had sung a hymn, Deacon began his lecture on the rich man who passed through the needle's eye before the camel with the Master's help. "We are blessed, brothers and sisters," Deacon proclaimed. "We are healthy and safe from the reanimated dead, the Teeth, we have enough to eat through all of our hard work. We truly are blessed. We should all be proud of each other, but humble ourselves…"

Deacon preached on and on about the beauty of out little homestead for a long time. "And most of all, the Great Master redeems the worst of us. Take for example Suzannah Commons." He looked directly at me; right when I thought it was all over. "Stand up, Suzannah."

"Telly," Silas whispered. "Telly, come here."

Telly climbed out of my lap and got into her brother's. I stood, wondering when they'd ever stop singling me out. I hung my head.

"You're penitent, aren't you?" Deacon asked.

I nodded.

"Come up here," he said. "Come to the front, daughter." I climbed over Silas's legs and walked up the aisle with everybody staring at me.

"Suzannah," Deacon said. He took my face in his hands and brought it up to look into his. His breath smelled like rotten meat. "Suzannah, do you want forgiveness?"

"Yes, Deacon," I answered.

"Then are you willing to be baptized and cleansed of your sins?"

I had been baptized several times in my life, this was nothing new. We all got baptized on a yearly basis.

"Come here, child," he said, guiding me to the baptismal font. I knew the water was already freezing. If it wasn't so snowy and wet outside, he'd take me to the river and baptize me there. "My child, do you repent from your sins?"

"Yes, Deacon, I do."

"Then go, submerse yourself in the water and arise as clean as the freshly driven snow."

I did as he asked, although the water was bone-chillingly cold. I arose from the water shivering and the congregation applauding. I glanced up and saw the hard labor girls glaring down at me with intense hatred in their eyes. "Welcome back to the community, daughter. You are a great example for the impure women of this commune. Everyone, she is redeemed for her sins, I ask you to not make an example of her any longer and to welcome her as long as she completes her tasks to become a wife. As it should be."

CHAPTER 6

We were dismissed back to our quarters, but I had to clean for Silas. I was shaking from the cold and my wet clothing.

"Mama! Papa! I'm clean!" I cried as the congregation was dismissed.

"You are no child of mine," Papa said, eyes narrowing.

"But, Papa…"

Papa and Mother turned their backs on me, and I was horrified. My siblings followed suit.

Something soft and warm was placed over my shoulders, it was Goody Maars putting her shawl on me. "Come with us, Suzannah," Dr. Maars said. My own parents turned their faces from me as I passed by, despite Deacon's insistence that I be accepted back into the community. They hated me. I hoped I could please them again someday. "It's not your fault they are behaving this way.

All I could think about was how much I had failed. How much I had disgraced our family tree. How disgusting was I for my parents to turn from me?

"No," I whispered. "It is."

Dr. Maars didn't respond to that. "Come with us." I followed them to the quarters and got out the cleaning tools from the cleaning closet down the hallway. When I came in, the white noise machine was on.

"I get migraines," Goody Maars said, sitting on the couch when I stopped to listen. The quarters were cold right now; the furnace had been shut off for the commune. Dr. Maars and Silas were setting soaking the wood in some kind of fluid before putting it into the cast iron stove.

"I have dry clothes you can change into," Goodwife Maars said.

"Here?" I asked, surprised.

"No, in my bedroom," she said. In her bedroom, she laid out a skirt and a tunic for me to change into on the bed. "This should help the cold. I'm surprised they didn't have fresh clothes for you to change into. You can get so sick if you walk around wet in the cold."

Once I changed, I gathered up the damp clothing and put it into the laundry sack. I'd sneak it in later tomorrow. "Thank you for giving me these."

"I couldn't let you catch a cold, could I?" she said. "I'm a doctor's wife, I understand this is how girls get sick in the winter. You don't know how many times I've had sick girls from the Handmaiden House come to the infirmary because they have infected sores from the lice bites and colds and frozen toes and fingertips and water in the lungs. Let's warm up in the other room."

Silas and Dr. Maars were setting the fire up to heat the room in the small wood stove. They removed a split log from a bucket of fluid, putting it into the iron stove oven, and Dr. Maars threw a lit match onto it.

It blazed to life. I jumped back.

"Everything alright?" Goody asked me.

"Which room is Silas's?" I stuttered, remembering why I was here.

"My room is the second on the right," Silas said.

I nodded. "Thank you."

Noah was waiting on the lower bunk. "What are you doing?" he asked, playing with wooden cars, racing them.

"Part of my punishment is to clean," I said, thinking of the pain of my parents turning from me. "So I'm cleaning your room."

"Yay!" he cried. "I don't have to do it anymore!"

"Noah," Goody said, sticking her head in the room. "She's not your slave, understand? One day soon you'll be cleaning this room again."

"Yes, Mother," Noah muttered.

"Come into the living room, leave her alone."

I continued and Noah left with his mother. My mind wasn't on what was Noah and what was Silas's. In my haste and distress at my parent's behavior towards me, I put the soiled clothing in a laundry sack and began putting toys back into the toy box, without worrying what was whose.

As I was sweeping the floor, Silas opened the door. "I've been calling you. I guess you can't hear me over the white noise machine. I just wanted to let you know the fire's going if you wanted to warm up," Silas said.

I hadn't finished the room, yet. "Okay," I said meekly.

In the living room, I held my numb fingers out to the cast iron stove for a moment. A blanket was put onto my shoulders. I whirled around in surprise to see Silas. "You had to be cold after that baptism," he said.

I nodded. "Thank you for letting me warm up."

"We're not animals, are we?" Dr. Maars commented. "I'd be a very bad doctor if I let you get sick."

"People get baptized every day in the winter. I've been very bad, lost part of my purity, this is part of my punishment," I responded. I knew that's what I was supposed to believe. I had to believe it. A set of fingers slipped under my chin and lifted my face.

"How many times do we have to tell you that you're not a bad person, Suzannah?" Dr. Maars said, looking right into my eyes. I shivered: men never did this to me unless I was edging towards punishment. "Mistakes don't make you a bad person."

I dipped my chin, and hung my head, putting my gaze back on the floorboards in shame.

"I'm sorry you have to walk all the way out to the Handmaiden House," Dr. Maars continued, "in this cold."

"I'll be fine," I admitted, shivering slightly.

"I have a spare set of clothing, if you'd like to change into something dry," Goody offered. "It's laid out on my bed in my room. You're welcome to it."

"Oh, I couldn't," I said.

"Stay and warm up," Dr. Maars said, picking something up. I realized it was a thick square, and the outsides were leather, and it opened.

It was a book! My jaw dropped. He began to read to his family by firelight.

People here didn't have books, except by special permission, and Deacon was always the one to grant them. Most of the time, it was the Elders. I realized the one he was reading from was different.

"Go, change clothes. You'll catch your death of cold," Goody said. "We'll let yours dry and you can take him to the laundry tomorrow night."

I reluctantly went back to her bedroom and changed into the tunic and long skirt. I hung my wet clothing up on the towel bar to dry.

Back in the living room, Dr. Maars was reading by

the lantern light. Telly climbed all over him and he held her still as he read.

"…Follow the yellow brick road…"

I looked at them. All of his children and his wife were sitting on the floor by the iron stove listening to him.

"What are you doing?" I asked, interrupting. "What are you reading?"

"I have access to the library," Dr. Maars said. "This is what my family does."

I watched suspiciously. "Only Deacon has books."

"I'm allowed to borrow the other ones," he said. "Would you like to listen?"

"Maybe tomorrow night," I said cautiously. He wasn't an Elder, let alone the Deacon. Was he really the right kind of person to read and interpret a book?

"It's a secret," Silas said. "Suzannah, I'd like it if you'd stay."

He was giving me an order. I had to stay. I was waiting for the trick that would do me in. I had to be obedient. "If you wish," I said, finally. "I'll stay."

Staying in my spot by the fire with my toes towards the flames, I kept the blanket wrapped around me. I didn't pay attention to what Dr. Maars was reading; he wasn't Deacon and he didn't have a chair on the Elder's council, I shouldn't listen to him at all, only Deacon. The fire was hotter and was burning much more slowly that how it did at the Handmaiden House, I realized. The flames were blue. I wondered how they had done this; it was obviously the fluid they had been soaked in.

Goody Maars came back into the room with the laundry sack and the cleaning bucket, and handed them to me.

"You best get back to the Handmaiden House, Suzannah," she said. "It's getting late."

"Yes, Goody."

"Just a moment," she said, taking the stones that had been heating on the stove top. "Take these in your pockets, it will keep you warm."

"Thank you," I said.

"Good night. Children, it's time to get to bed."

"Oh!" I cried.

"Yes?"

"Silas?" I asked. "What would you like to eat in the morning?"

He gave me a lop-sided smile. "Whatever everybody else is eating."

The days continued similarly to my first day practicing my work as a wife. I had heard people say that I was already servicing Silas like a whore and that I was no longer a virgin. To be honest, I didn't quite know what virginity was, asides from a status that Deacon gave and took away.

One older girl in the Handmaiden House, Kaffrey, a cousin of mine, was getting married. The news went around the commune at dinnertime. "Suzannah, you go and see to Kaffrey," Silas said. "Don't stop by my quarters, I won't tell anyone."

"We won't, either," Goody Maars said.

"I'll come by later," I said.

"No, it's fine," Dr. Maars said. "We won't say anything."

"I'll clean up after dinner," Goody said.

After I finished dinner, I followed the girls from the Handmaiden House, lagging behind. They were so excited for Kaffrey, and were giggling and chatting, but not including me. I crossed the threshold and the House

Matron sent us on errands: I was sent to obtain an extra set of towels from the laundry. When I came back, I saw Kaffrey, sitting the steel, steaming bathing tub with the House Matron scrubbing her down. A group of girls were assisting with washing her. The others were sitting nearby because of the warmth the hot water was putting out, another group of girls, who had been heating water over the fire, were carrying another bucket of hot water to pour onto Kaffrey.

"But what do I?" Kaffrey asked, looking white as a sheet. "Nobody will tell me!"

"Don't be afraid," the House Matron said stiffly. "Whatever happens tonight won't be as bad as what happens to the labor whores. If you're nice to him, he'll be nice to you."

"But what do you mean by 'nice'?" Kaffrey asked, wide-eyed.

"Heavenly Stars above, child!" the House Matron spat, scrubbing her hair roughly. She cried out at how hard she was being scrubbed. "Do you want to be hard labor whore or a wife? Which one?"

"A wife! A wife!" Kaffrey cried. The Matron pushed her under the water roughly and pulled her back up, her hair free of the soap suds.

"Oakley?" the Matron asked.

Oakley was standing nearby with a large bath towel and Kaffrey stood up, naked, and Oakley wrapped her up in the towel immediately.

"Girls, I expect her hair to be braided neatly and out of her face," the Matron said, wiping her hands on her apron. "The rose lotion and the flowers are on the bedside table beside her bed. Simber, Suzannah, Blossom, and Essie, all of you dump this tub outside once it's cooled off."

"Yes, ma'am," we all said, casting our eyes to the ground.

She walked out of the room to her private quarters.

The rest of us girls took turns getting out the lotion and pouring some into our hands. It smelled nice, like flowers, I supposed that was an extra touch for our husbands to enjoy. I wondered what her soon-to-be-husband was doing right now.

I sniffed the rose scent again. We didn't have a lot of flowers in the commune, though. This was an extravagance. Emmy, one of the best hair braiders in the Handmaiden House, took to braiding Kaffrey's hair while it was wet. We rubbed her arms, legs, and back down with the lotion. I didn't mind the nice scent of roses on me.

"What do you think is going to happen to me?" Kaffrey said, her eyes wide with panic.

"Everything will be fine," Simber said. "Stop being such a baby about it."

"I've heard it hurts," Blossom said. "My older sister said so when she got married. She wouldn't tell me how she said it's a secret."

"Maybe Suzannah knows," Essie sneered.

"I don't know anything!" I snapped.

"Don't touch me, whore," Kaffrey snapped. I realized she was speaking to me. "Get away from me, I don't need your filth on me on my marriage night. Besides, don't you have to go and service Silas Maars?"

I hung my head in shame as all the other girls turned their backs of me and started putting flowers in Kaffrey's hair, giggling at her remark. Even Simber and Oakley were disregarding me and had smirks on their faces, now. Tears of shame flooded my vision and my cheeks burned.

I brushed back my tears; she was right, I did need to go clean Silas's room now that dinner was over, even if the Maarses weren't expecting me.

I put my shawl over my shoulders and trudged back outside, wiping my tears away. I wondered if there would be anyone to help me prepare for my marriage if everyone was still calling me a whore and filthy, or would I eventually go to the hard labor camp anyway? Who'd dress me, braid my hair, and bathe me on marriage night? No one, I was certain.

The fire was already blazing in the Maars' quarters. "Hello, Suzannah," Goody said. "Is Kaffrey ready to be married?"

"She's ready," I said numbly, avoiding her eyes. "Excuse me, Goody."

In Silas's room, all of Noah's toys were put away and the laundry was in a neat pile in the corner. I gathered it up and stuffed it into the laundry sack. Silas climbed onto the top bunk of the bed and watched me.

I felt so angry that everybody thought I was a bad person because Silas had told on me, but the Maars kept on insisting I wasn't one. Why had be told? Why did the Maarses have to be so confusing and contradictory? I was so frustrated; I couldn't even come up with the words!

"Can I help you?" Silas asked.

"No," I said icily. "You've done enough. Are you going to tell Deacon that you cleaned up before I got here because you thought I wasn't coming?"

"Why would I do that?" Silas asked. "Maybe I like putting my dirty laundry in one spot and not all over the room. And we said..."

"Then why did you tell on me?"

"I wasn't the one," he snapped. When he snapped, I

wasn't sure why he didn't hit me, too. I paused.

"Are you sure?"

"Yes, I'm sure. It was an accident; I didn't see any need to tell."

"I committed a sin, I have to take the punishment," I said irritably, putting a few of Noah's toys back into the toy box.

All I could think of was Momma and Papa turning on me because of him. He was silent while I continued putting the toys away.

"Was it really a sin or just an accident?"

"It was both."

"Wouldn't I have sinned too? Not locking the door? Wouldn't I be responsible for you seeing me?"

How in the world was it his fault?

"I can't believe you'd do something accidentally and blame yourself," he continued. I realized I had stopped what I was doing. "I'm partially to blame if it's a sin. It was an accident. The Great Master understands it wasn't anybody's fault."

Men were never to blame when it came to purity-related sins. It was the woman's fault, always, for tempting them. Our bodies had more power than we realized, Deacon said, and we were responsible for what it did to men. "I blame myself and I'm sorry," I said, lowering my eyes. "That's what accidents are."

"It was nobody's fault. I was just in the wrong place at the wrong time."

I worked in silence for a few more minutes, scrubbing the broken tile floor with mop water, thinking of my sins, destroying my parent's love for me.

"Why didn't you hit me just now?"

"Because hitting doesn't make me right. It just hurts you long enough to make you quiet. For a while."

"You need to learn. Wives need that to know when they're wrong."

"Suzannah, hitting doesn't help."

"Then how else do you learn when you're wrong?"

"Your conscience."

I had heard Deacon mention the conscience before, but he said that women didn't have them, they were not developed enough like men were. That's why we had to be covered up at all times: we didn't know how seductive our bodies were.

"It's that voice inside your head that tells you were wrong. Like when you saw me naked and looked away," Silas said.

I had looked away. I had been so upset with myself. Did this mean I was equal enough to Silas that I had a conscience?

"I saw you do it," he said. "You didn't stare."

I knelt, and considered what he was saying. I *had* looked away. I did it because… I knew it was wrong to look. "I did because… it was your privacy. I didn't want to invade it… I knew."

"See?"

I shook my head, frustrated. "I'm a girl, I can't have that thing…"

"You have a conscience; it exists in you. Just because you can't see it doesn't mean it's not there. Like the Ruins. You've never been to The Ruins."

"What are 'The Ruins' anyway?" I asked, even more irritated. There was no way I had a conscience. I needed a man to teach me and regulate me. I couldn't handle the choice between right and wrong, I was only a girl. "A deserted commune like ours, just falling apart? It's useless and nobody lives there, except for maybe the cannibals, they'll eat us alive…"

"They're much more than a commune! It was a great city a long time ago. With no fences. Where men *and* women used to live before the flood and they came and went as they pleased."

"I've never been outside the commune," I responded. He watched me clean the windows with vinegar water, which angered me even more. "Why don't you tell me what to make for your meals?" I asked, trying to get him off the subject.

"Because I don't see the benefit in making you work harder than you have to," he said. "You're already tired everyday. I can see it in your face."

"Don't you get tired from militia training? Everybody's tired around here. If we don't work, we don't survive."

"That's a different kind of tired. I get an adequate amount of time to sleep. You don't."

"So what if I don't sleep? How is that your problem?"

"It's not but… I'm sort of… in charge of you. Deacon wants me to be anyway."

"Then why aren't you bossing me around? Smacking me for talking to you when I should be working?"

"I don't think anybody should be in charge of another," he said quietly. He was silent for a long time and I turned around to look at him. He was staring at me with his jaw dropped from the top bunk of the bed. "I don't think it's okay to hit someone, even if it's your wife. I don't believe in laying my hands on anybody who hasn't hit me first. I don't think that women should have to do whatever their husbands say, either. My father doesn't do those things to my mother, even when she upsets him. Why should I do it to you?"

There was nothing but shock at this admission. I had witnessed his family's odd behavior over meals before, but never put excessive thought into it. They were just strange. I assumed they were just like everybody else when I wasn't around. "Because… the man is the head of the household!" I cried. "The woman is meant to submit to the man, we were made second by the Master and inferior, that's why you fight in the militia and we stay at home. We're not very smart!"

"Women used to fight in the militia."

"They did not!" I cried, horrified.

"They did too," he said. "I've got photography to prove it."

My jaw dropped. "Where?" I had seen photography, but there wasn't much left. The teachers showed us photographs and drawings in school, but it was because Deacon allowed them to. I crossed my arms: he was attempting to make a fool of me.

"I saw it in a book."

"You did not!"

"I'll get it. For tomorrow night, I'll show you the picture then." He hopped off the top bunk.

"I don't believe you. Everybody calls you queer, I think your family's queer, too!"

Silas's jaw dropped. "Do you even know what that means, Suzannah?"

"That's you're weird. You're all weird. Women don't know or understand what men can understand. Men know best. That's why your father's the doctor and your mother's only the goodwife."

"That term means something other than 'weird,'" he said darkly. "Something much worse."

"Maybe I'm not supposed to understand what it means," I said.

"You'll understand once you're married," Silas snorted. "I'm going to get that book and show you."

I shrugged and walked out of the room to see Goody Maars sitting beside the fire with Dr. Maars. Telly was in her lap, asleep, and Noah was leaning on her. I sneaked out of their quarters. I had to see Kaffrey get married.

All I could think of was how strange it was that women had once been in the militia and that airplanes were real and that Dr. Maars didn't strike his wife. Most of the Elders did, I had seen them do it. Other Elders encouraged them. My own father did it when he was angry with my mother and with me and my siblings for doing things that displeased him. Deacon even talked about how in the Holy Book, the Great Master encouraged the rod against women who were out of line and out of control. I couldn't count how many women I had witnessed getting lashed in the courtyard. I didn't know how the Maars managed their household when Dr. Maars didn't control his wife. Women couldn't be trusted to stay in control, Deacon said so.

But I had turned from looking at Silas. Something, deep inside me, had told me it was wrong. And Deacon said women didn't have a conscience. But, strangely, I did. How was that possible? What was wrong with me? Was I part boy and didn't know it? Was I deformed and wrong and should have been left to die as a baby? Would I be cast out into the labor fields if I were to marry and my husband find out? I was terrified that this was true.

In the worship hall, I just got there in time to walk in with Kaffrey, who looked beautiful, but scared. She had been sent through the "maidening," a ceremony that the Matrons did for the girls from the Handmaiden House about to marry, a moment when they all encircled her, laid hands upon her and begged the Great Master to make her fertile and obedient for her new husband.

"You're back early," Oakley said.

"I know," I said. "I'm getting faster."

"It must be nice," Oakley commented sympathetically.

"It's not nice!" Simber snapped, turning around to glare at her. "How stupid are you? It's embarrassing for her! She should be ashamed of what she's having to do!"

"Okay. If you say so," Oakley muttered.

I stared at the cockroach that scuttled across the floor.

"Kaffrey? You can go, now. Your parents are in the chapel," a House Matron said.

She walked out, ahead of us, trembling. The Sub-Elder she was marrying stood at the end of the aisle with his other wife, who was glaring at her. We walked in behind them and sat down in the pews. Everyone edged away from me, even Simber and eventually, Oakley, too.

I tried not to think about it as we watched Kaffrey be married. Deacon was still wearing his robe and stole from worship. I wondered how Kaffrey was taking it.

"Kaffrey Commons, are you ready to be a subservient wife to Elder Thomas, and to bear his children?" Deacon asked.

"I am," she uttered, pale under the veil shielding her face

"Thomas, you now have a wife to take under your wing. Do you take her for a wife?"

"I do."

"Then I pronounce you married. You may take her, now."

"Thank you, Deacon. As it should be."

The older man kissed Deacon's hand, and then Kaffrey had her turn.

"Go, and make the commune grow. As it should be."

The older man took Kaffrey by the arm and they walked down the aisle together. I saw her shaking.

"Now that the marriage ceremony is complete, you young girls are welcome to go back to the Handmaiden House for the night. May your marriages be soon. As it should be," Deacon said.

"As it should be," we all repeated in unison.

"You are dismissed."

The next night after dinner, I went to the Maars' quarters to clean Silas's room. "I got it," Silas said.

"You got what?" I saw a book in his lap. It was a giant book, covered in pictures. I had seen pictures before, but they were in school. They were rare, we didn't have the technology to make photographs anymore. The book said LIFE in large white letters. "Silas!" I cried. "What are you doing with that? You know you'll get in trouble if they find out you have it!"

"No, I won't," he said. "They don't even notice if we keep it hidden."

"Books are rare!"

"No, they're not," he chuckled. "They've got a whole room full of books in the Elders' wing. On shelves and stacked on top of each other in giant piles."

"A whole room?" I repeated, trying to imagine it. "Is that where you got these?"

"Yeah," he said, flipping through the book. "There's thousands of books. Tens of thousands. Maybe even a hundred thousand!"

"You're making that up," I said.

"Here." He showed me a beautiful printed page. It had yellowed a bit, the edges were dog-eared. I felt a chill; I never was allowed to handle something as precious as a book before. I had learned to read by a chalkboard and it helped when there were directions painted on the walls of the laundry and the directions on the cooking cards. This was special and sacred, and Silas was letting me handle it like the bag of laundry I picked up every night. I looked at the page on the book: in the middle, a picture was in black and white of a group of women dressed in pantsuits, like the mechanics in our commune, standing by some large metal thing. They were grinning, proud, brandishing tools, not ashamed to be forced into wearing pants like the hard labor whores were forced to, their hair under colorful red patterned bandanas.

Women Airforce Service Pilots (WASPs)

I blinked. "Real women in the militia?" I asked.

"Yeah. They used to have a militia with an entire department where they flew airplanes."

"Airplanes are made-up."

"They used to drop bombs on the enemies during wars. They'd blow up entire cities. And shoot each other down in air fights."

"Men can't fly," I snorted.

"I've flown."

"You're making that up, you have not. It's impossible!"

"They used to know how," he said. "Papa says that there are people that still know. People go to places to get onto planes called *aeroports*. And the pilots would drive them across the world. You've never read a book, have you?"

I bit my lower lip and finally shook my head. "No, I haven't. You're trying to make a fool of me."

"No, I'm not," he said. "How could I fake this?"

I stared at the picture and thought about it. He couldn't fake pictures like this.

"I'd never try to trick you, Suzannah. I'm telling the truth."

Silas left me alone, leaving the door open, the book in my lap.

I scoured it, drinking in the information, trying to read the page.

So much information. So much to learn! I wanted to memorize every page. Deacon would never know, and I'd have secret knowledge. Maybe one day, I could use it!

It was getting late, and I finally put the book away, although I wanted to keep reading it. I finished with cleaning the floor and got out some fresh sheets from the laundry. I hated making up Silas's bed because it was on the top bunk and I couldn't stand on the floor to do it, so I had to stand on the bed. I worried that I'd get the lice from the Handmaiden House on Silas's sheets.

I walked out to the living room, to see if Goody Maars was going to be true to her word.

"Goodwife Maars?" I asked. "Can I speak to you?"

She got up from the couch where her husband was sitting by the fireplace. "Is something wrong?"

"No," I said quietly. "I'm just… I'm afraid I've got lice again and I've got to make Silas's bed…"

"I understand," she said. "I was in the Handmaiden House, too, for a long time. Silas can make his own bed. Come now, we're going to listen to another story."

"No, I'm not going to stop doing my punishment."

"You're tired, and it would be a shame to miss it."

"No, I'm not going to!" I pleaded. "I'll be punished more! Sent to the hard labor camp! What about that delousing spray you had in the infirmary? Do you have any more? Please?"

"That takes a day or so to work, dear," she said. "I understand how poorly they treat the girls in the

Handmaiden House. Did you know that I almost aged out? I almost got sent to the hard labor camp myself?"

I wondered how she became a Goodwife instead. I knew it would be rude to ask.

"I know Silas showed you a book tonight, didn't he?"

I nodded reluctantly.

"Please don't tell anybody he has it. We get books from the library, Silas asked his father to get that one for him. He borrowed it, Deacon doesn't know."

"I won't tell."

"Maybe sometime you can take a hot shower in our bathroom instead of cleaning," she offered. "I know you don't have heated water in the Handmaiden House, and you don't have to clean every night. Silas can do it for himself. That's partially Noah's mess, too."

I hadn't had a hot shower in all the time I had lived in the Handmaiden House. The bath I had gotten in the infirmary had been too nice, yet she had never reported it. "No," I said. "They'd know."

"Maybe not," she said. "Now go on."

I gathered up the last of the laundry and went on. I wondered why she was so kind to me.

CHAPTER 7

The weeks passed and the weather warmed up. I was able to wash again in the mornings and Goodwife Maars helped me delouse. I felt so much better when I didn't smell so badly and itch all the time.

I'd come to the Maars quarters and often times find Silas and Noah's room already clean, the beds made, and the laundry gathered. I usually listened to Dr. Maars read while I was working after chapel. Tonight was no different.

"Can I just take these back to the Handmaiden House and return them tomorrow?" I asked, going into the living room with the laundry sack. So far, I hadn't been told on for some reason.

"Why don't you stay?" Silas asked.

"No, I really shouldn't," I said, casting my eyes down to the cracked tiles. A few roaches scattered to the baseboards.

"I wish you could, Suzannah," Dr. Maars said, looking up from his book. "I'm reading to the family again."

"What are you reading?" I asked, fascinated.

"*Treasure Island*."

I had heard the word *treasure*, but not *island* before.

"What's an island?"

"It's a small bit of land, surrounded by the ocean," Telly said. "The pirates buried a treasure chest with diamonds and gold and rubies and emeralds and... Will you sit with me, Suzannah?"

I took a seat beside Telly, and instead, she climbed into my lap. I liked holding her, though, especially during worship. My own mother had told me to sit somewhere else with my reputation and damaged purity during worship. My parents pretended I didn't exist, I was now completely parentless. But this child wanted me to hold her and her parents didn't mind. I felt my heart swell.

"...His stories were what frightened people worst of all. Dreadful stories they were— about hanging, and walking the plank, and stores at sea, and the Dry Tortugas, and wild deeds and places on the Spanish Main..."

I listened to Dr. Maars read the book. It was the most exciting thing I had ever heard. I had heard the stories of the Great Warrior who helped His people out of bondage by killing the Pharaoh in battle during worship a million times and when he overcame Pontius Pilate with a mighty rod that he fashioned from a whip to drive him out of the temple, but this was completely different. This was the story of a boy named Jim who went on a ship that sailed the seas to find gold and silver to get his mother out of debt. How brave. How loving. How valiant a son. I hoped I had a son like this someday, who loved me this much, so I didn't end up a Matron, rejected by her husband for a younger, more fertile girl from the Handmaiden House.

"What happened to Jim?" I asked. "And his mother? Did she ever remarry?"

"You'll have to find out tomorrow night," Dr. Maars said, a smile growing underneath his beard. He shut the book.

"But did he go on to marry and have children? Are his children here in the commune? Did they survive the Great Flood?"

The Maarses looked a bit surprised. "Suzannah, this is fiction. It's a story that isn't real. It never happened," he said.

"So it's a lie? We're not supposed to lie!"

"No, not a lie, just something Robert Louis Stevenson made up for other people to read and enjoy."

"What happened to Robert Louis Stevenson?"

"I don't know," Dr. Maars answered, shrugging.

"This is what books are," Silas explained. "Stories made up by other people to entertain those who read it."

"So everybody *knows* he's lying?"

Dr. Maars looked over to Goody Maars and they exchanged a smile. "It's not a lie if you explain it's not real beforehand," Dr. Maars said. "We'll read the rest tomorrow. It's time for everyone to get to bed," he said.

"I need to get your laundry," I said, standing up.

I went into Silas's room and gathered the laundry sack in the corner. "Mother made Noah and me clean up our room," Silas said from the doorway.

"Thank you, but you shouldn't do that," I said. "They'll find out."

"They don't know that we borrow so many books from the library," Silas said. "How would they know that you listen to us read instead?"

Silas insisted he hadn't told on me when I saw him naked. I had to believe him at this point. I decided I owed the Maars family this secret. "What's this library thing you always talk about?"

"The room where they keep the books. We have access to it; they just don't know we do take them back to our quarters."

"That's like stealing," I said. "Stealing is wrong; Deacon says so."

"But we put it back. Besides, Deacon expects Mother and Papa to borrow books from there. They have lots and lots of books on illnesses and medicines. They help them keep people alive."

"That sounds like witchcraft. The Master forbids it."

"He forbids using *magic*. What my parents do isn't magic, it's *science*. It saves people's lives. There's no witchery involved."

"But stop the time when the Master says that it's time for people to die?"

"How do you know what the Master says? You're only human. Besides, the Master left science for us to know how to do things and discover the secrets of the world."

"You're wrong. Questioning is wrong."

"The nice thing about science is that it's true, regardless of if you believe in it or not."

"I know you're wrong because I listen to Deacon. Deacon is close to the Master; he tells us what to do because he hears it from the Master directly. Maybe the Master doesn't want us experimenting with stuff we shouldn't know about."

"The Master *speaking* to him? Why doesn't the Master just speak to all of us instead? Why doesn't Master speak to *you*?"

"He doesn't speak to me because I'm a girl!"

"The Master's talked to girls all through history

through his angels. The Prophetess Deborah, Rebecca, Edith, Ruth, the Virgin Mary..."

"He doesn't talk to women."

"Yeah, He did. Through His angels. It's in the Holy Book."

I was stumped.

"The Holy Book?"

"Yeah. I've read it. There's a few of them under lock and key in Deacon's office. But there are also some in the library. That's where Deacon gets all his lectures from. He just changes the stories a little bit to convince people he can't be wrong. He is, sometimes."

I stuffed the last of his dirty clothes into the laundry bag and punched it a few times to stuff them down. "Doesn't it bother you that I've seen you without any clothes on? And I'm always around?"

He shrugged. "Well, it was embarrassing, but... you know, that's like the statues in The Ruins."

"You keep claiming The Ruins are so amazing and so wonderful."

"They are. I wouldn't lie to you."

I realized he hadn't; at least, I thought he hadn't. Maybe I wasn't smart enough to tell if the Maarses lied about things. "Are they like the statue we have of the Great Warrior? In the courtyard?" I asked finally.

"Yeah, I've seen them. They're naked."

I gasped. "No! You shouldn't look, then! That's horrible! People just see them all day long without any clothes on?"

"It's beautiful. It's the human body. I'm not ashamed of my body."

"Why not?"

"It's not that I like to walk around naked or anything, but I'm normal. We were born naked, you know. And

Adam and Eve were naked in the Garden of Eden before they ate the apple."

"No, all of his wives forced him to eat it and tricked him. That's why we're supposed to be afraid of being naked in front of others. Unless we're married. It causes us to think impure thoughts; to sin. That's why I sinned when I saw you!"

He shrugged. "Accidents happen."

"Why were you in your quarters that day? Instead of at drill with the others in the militia, like you were supposed to be?"

"I fell. Into the mud. They sent me to the quarters to shower and get cleaned up, that's why. Besides, it was a little embarrassing when you walked in, but there's nothing wrong with me. Is there something wrong with you?"

My jaw dropped. "No! I don't think so…" I wondered sometimes if I were normal under my clothes at times. My new-found fear that the reason I had a conscience was because I was part boy resurfaced again. But Goody Maars had told me there was nothing wrong with me, so I had to be normal. But she was a woman, not a man. She couldn't be right. What was really wrong with me? "No, I'm sure I'm normal. And you shouldn't be asking me questions like that!"

"Mother is smart enough. She's a woman, too you know. She knows when something is normal or abnormal. Better than Papa even, sometimes."

"Then she's really special to be smarter than your father," I said sarcastically.

"No, she's not really. She just read a lot of books. There's a journal you know. One a doctor made of the human form, showing where all the internal organs were, the capillaries, the veins, the arteries. Wanna see?"

"It sounds disgusting."

"It's only drawings. It's in the library. I saw it once when I was younger, my parents got to bring it home to study."

"That's horrible!"

"Mother and Papa are better at their jobs because of it," he offered. "They save lives."

"Maybe the Master doesn't want them to save lives," I said. "Maybe the Master is calling them to allow people to die and they're sinning by keeping them alive instead!"

"All life is important, Suzannah. My mother and sister are just as important as my brother and father and me. You're important, you're not replaceable. You're you."

His words hit me like a rock to the head. I was trying to push him away because he seemed too interested in me. Nobody had ever called me important before; we weren't as smart; we were wild and unstable at times. We needed the men in this commune to help control us and provide for us. His words made my head spin. I was so confused, I burst into tears. "Why do you say things like that, Silas? It'll only get you in trouble!"

I went to storm out, but Goodwife Maars grabbed my shoulder. "Suzannah, don't go out there like that," she said. "Come on, let's wash your face." She took me to her bathroom and ran some water, wetting it down a cloth. "Did Silas say something to you?"

"He's saying things he shouldn't," I said, sniffling.

"Suzannah, let me tell you something," she said softly. "You've probably noticed our family is different. We *are* different."

My jaw dropped and she washed my face gently.

"Please don't tell the others this. Deacon knows about it, and as long as we keep it quiet, he doesn't mind."

"It's because Dr. Maars so close in age to you, isn't it?"

She sighed. "That might be part of it, yes," she said, getting a dry towel to pat the water off my face. "The way my husband treats me is dangerous to the rest of the commune. He treats me as an equal. You see, Suzannah, the truth is that men and women are different, but we're equals. We're strong in different ways. We're equal in our strengths and weaknesses. In some ways, I'm strong, in others, it's Ephraim that's the strong one. We depend on each other to be stronger together. Ephraim and I… we're equals in the infirmary."

"How?" I asked.

"'How' what?"

"How do you mean you're equals?"

"We're equals in that we agree on matters. Ephraim, if he could do anything, would paint pictures all day and draw, but he knows medicine and science, too. But he asks me for my opinion because he misses things in the infirmary. I have an intuition as to what things mean, what they indicate, and how to treat the problems. I was taught at a young age to read medical charts and tests, to run labs, to diagnose what they mean and what medications to give. It's what I dream about, my purpose in life, it's a passion for me. The ways of the body, when it's not right, just *speak* to me. They do as well for Ephraim, but not as much. Don't mistake me, he knows a lot. There are moments Ephraim refers to me, he'll do what I tell him to do, he trusts me and does what I insist is right. He gets all the credit from Deacon, though. When people ask, Ephraim claims he runs the infirmary to cover for me. If the people in this commune knew I run things, we'd be burned alive in the courtyard together."

I shivered at the thought: a woman had been burned

alive five winters ago for killing one of her other sister wives with poison. It had been terrifying to watch. I swore I'd never hurt my sister wives, should I have any, and I'd be a good wife when the time came. "I know I already agree on everything my husband will tell me to do."

"Yes, but sometimes, Ephraim needs my knowledge. I was the oldest of the old doctor's children. I shadowed him since age eight. I read the books and I was able to predict what my father would do the best of all. Ephraim was brought in when he showed the most aptitude, but when we operate, it's me that knows best. I think, if you are careful enough, there's a chance you could marry Silas. Silas likes you."

"He doesn't act like it."

"He just annoys you because he doesn't know how else to talk to you. But he wants to talk to you, dear."

"I don't know that I want an equal for a husband. I don't know how to make decisions."

"You do. Try it sometime. Here." She pulled a handkerchief out of her pocket and handed it to me. I unwrapped it; it was a small heart-shaped bread. It was hard, but there was something pink and jelly-like in the middle. "Your feelings aren't wrong, no matter what anybody tries to convince you. This is for you. It's to eat. Try eating it by yourself, you don't want others asking where you got it."

"Thank you," I muttered, although I didn't know what it was.

"Have a good night. I'll see you tomorrow."

I took the little piece of food and sniffed it on the way back to the Handmaiden House. It smelled sweet and like strawberries. We had had strawberries last summer. They had been tart, but really sweet. I saw the men in the guard tower with their guns watching me cross the courtyard, so I stuffed it back into my pocket, wrapped in the handkerchief.

In the Handmaiden House, I took the handkerchief and hid it under my blanket. I put on my nightdress and climbed into the bed, looking at Kaffrey's empty bed down the way. There wasn't a new girl in the house to take her place, yet.

The Matron turned off the lights and told us to be quiet, it was time to sleep. I felt some pity for the next girl to get her cycle; I hadn't known what was wrong with me when the blood started, and mother made me get dressed and took me to the Handmaiden House. The Matron had shown me how to bundle the rags and tuck them into my undergarments. She allowed me to rest for the rest of the afternoon and checked on me repeatedly, explaining that I'd never get an afternoon off again, and I was no longer a child and unwelcome in my family's quarters. I cried myself to sleep that night, but I met Oakley and Simber when worship was over and the girls came back to the house. They had just started their cycles, too. They comforted me; Simber explained that we weren't expected to meet our quotas during the week that all the girls in the house cycled and Oakley brought some warm soup for me from the kitchens. It had only been about this time last year. Having friends made it easier. I wished I'd be able to do that for the next girl, but I knew there was no way possible.

I laid in bed, contemplating how Dr. and Goody Maars could possibly be equals. I sniffed the little cracker again and finally brought it to my mouth in the dark. It broke off between my teeth and it tasted as sweet as smelled. I closed my eyes; it was absolutely sinful. I chewed carefully and slowly, enjoying it.

When I had finished it, I wanted another one, but I realized I had wasted the only one I had.

I should have saved it for later. But I'd have never known it's sweetness unless I had taken that first bite.

I'd be more careful next time I got one and enjoy it. If I ever was given that opportunity.

CHAPTER 8

Suzannah!" Telly came running through the common room to me. "Hi, Telly," I said, picking her up. "Suzannah, did you like the cookie?"

"The what?"

"Shh," Goodwife Maars said. "That's something we don't tell everyone about. We don't have enough to share."

"It was very good," I admitted. "Thank you."

She smiled as we waited.

"What are they made from?" I whispered.

"Flour, sugar, salt, strawberries…"

Those were all rare ingredients, except the flour. We didn't get a lot of sugar here, and that which we did usually went to the men first. There was rarely any left for the women or girls. The strawberries were so small and tart, the men usually got them first.

As we waited on the men, I served Silas once Goodwife Maars was finished.

"Suzannah Commons."

I jumped and almost sloshed some protein mush on Silas. I whirled to see an Elder standing behind us.

"I see that Silas Maars isn't eating anything different from everyone else."

I choked and couldn't speak. I wasn't supposed to. My fear of becoming a hard labor whore was pounding a hole in my chest.

"Silas never asks for anything different," Dr. Maars said.

"We worry that she's not performing her punishment adequately."

"He insists that she have his laundry folded and ironed a certain way. She does an exemplary job with his room, and also cleans after Noah without being asked. You know how boys are; they make messes but don't like cleaning them up. Every night, Silas and Noah sleep on clean blankets and sheets, which I believe Silas prefers. I think she's doing well in her punishment. It's making her better wife material already."

The Elder stared at Dr. Maars and then me and back to Dr. Maars. "She's that good?"

"She is. All the work she's doing has helped my wife with her headaches. We appreciate having her assistance, Elder Dale."

"Suzannah?"

"Yes, sir?" I asked, keeping my eyes to the floor.

"This is good news to hear. You are redeeming your purity again."

I breathed a sigh of relief I hadn't realized I was holding when he walked away. Goodwife Maars placed a hand on my shoulder. "Everything's alright," she whispered in my ear. "You're always welcome in our family."

"You shouldn't lie for me. Or clean Silas and Noah's room so I can listen to your husband read. I'm going to do all the work tonight," I whispered.

"Nonsense, I don't clean Silas and Noah's room," she said. "Come on, the men are finished."

I sat down at the table and waited for Goodwife Maars to finish serving herself when she passed the bowl along to me. "Silas?" I asked, spooning out the mush. "Do you want anything special for lunchtime?"

"What everyone else is having," Silas said. I looked up and realized he was looking at me directly. He smiled at me and I felt something I hadn't expect: a fluttery feeling in the base of my stomach. I looked away quickly; I couldn't afford to feel this way, it was wrong. Deacon would surely find out. I couldn't afford to be any more wrong than I had already been.

After worship, I followed the Maars back to their quarters, feeling eager to hear what Dr. Maars was going to read next. I sat by the open window with Telly in my lap on the floor, braiding her hair while Dr. Maars continued with *Treasure Island.*

I wondered if anybody had ever been on a pirate ship, sailing the sea. I had heard of the sea, but what I had seen of it was dirty in pictures. The oil washed up on the shore in globs into the sand on brown water and the oil wells burned in the horizon. The sky was dark yellow and smoky. The people there were mutated and deformed, Deacon said they became the reanimated dead from the plague that made the water so disgusting. Those that didn't were the cannibals, or the "Teeth", who roamed the countryside, willing to eat human flesh. Dead animal skeletons lined the beaches.

But what Dr. Maars read was beautiful. I could see the clear blue water lapping white sand that was like piles of flour when I was making bread. I wondered if the sea was like this somewhere in real life.

It was dangerous to make things up in your mind.

Deacon said so. But if someone wrote this down, it must have happened. Was it making it up if some one saw it real life?

I shouldn't think such thoughts, I thought. It was too confusing.

The intercom rang and Goody Maars got up, putting down her knitting to answer it. "One of the girls in the labor camp is sick, she's requesting you," the guard on the intercom said.

Goody and the Doctor exchanged a worried glance.

"We'll be there soon," Dr. Maars said.

"What's going on?" I asked.

"A girl in the hard labor camp is having a baby," Dr. Maars said.

"I thought they didn't have babies," I said. "They're not married."

"You can have a baby when you're not married. The problem is, with lack of food and the diseases that go around the labor camp, their pregnancies don't always survive," Dr. Maars said, putting his jacket on. "Their babies usually die before they're born."

"I don't know of any of them that were currently pregnant," Goody said, getting her shawl on and sorting through their cabinets.

I felt like I had been punched in the stomach. "They do?" I whispered. "They're non-babies?"

"Yes. They get buried in the backfield."

Deacon said that non-babies were never welcome into Paradise. I felt sick. Non-babies were the children of the Darkman or the Teeth. They weren't human.

"I wonder if it's Dawn," Goody muttered, gathering items. We weren't to speak their names ever again once they were sent there. It was part of their punishment. "She hasn't let us examine her in a while."

"I think so," Dr. Maars said. "Silas, you're in charge until we get home."

"Yes, sir," Silas said.

"What's going on?" I asked. "How long are you going to be gone?"

"For however long this takes," Dr. Maars said.

Goody turned to me and stared at me as if studying me for a moment. "Suzannah, come with us."

I was shocked; she wanted me to go into the hard labor camp? I shook my head.

"Marisa, she's not ready for this," Dr. Maars whispered.

"Yes, she is. You need to see this," she said, handing me a blanket to use as a shawl. "You need to see what Deacon's system is creating."

"You're right. Suzannah, come with us," Dr. Maars commanded, opening the door. I was surprised he took Goody's advice and let her make a decision like this. I had to go, now.

My legs began to tremble as we walked down the hall together. In the infirmary, the Maars gathered supplies, including a bucket, handing it to me. I was too scared to go against what they told me to do, but I didn't want to see the camp. All those girls, so unclean… what would happen to me there?

I followed them outdoors. The searchlights had been turned off, and we crossed the courtyard in the dark, heading towards the tent. The tent was dark, except for two lanterns, and the girls were surrounding one of the others. They were all dirty and smelled bad, their hair shorn to their shoulders. A few of them turned to look at me, and I recognized only a few of them; many of them were missing their teeth and they had been beaten. They were nameless now. Their faces were bruised, making it harder for me to recognize them. They all looked at me with dead eyes. They were all so, so thin. I felt nauseated I was so scared. What would they do to me?

"Dr. Maars?" one of them asked. "She's over here."

The crowd parted and I saw a girl, who was gaunt and bony, except for her stomach, which was protruding slightly under her shirt, laying on a mattress. Her hair was wet and pulled back; she was soaked in sweat.

"Dawn!" Goody Maars cried. She rushed to her side and took her hand, pressing her own hand on the girl's bloated stomach. "Dawn, is this why you haven't let us examine you?"

Dawn nodded. This meant the Maars came here often.

Goody pulled her to her chest and held her. "Why didn't you tell me?"

"Because…" Dawn uttered through broken teeth. She tried to say something else, but I couldn't understand.

"It's nothing to worry about now," Dr. Maars said. "I want all of you to know, we're here to help you. *Anything* you need help with."

"Let me take care of you," Goody said, stroking her hair like she did for me. We weren't supposed to even touch these girls, they were so unclean, yet Goody was holding her like she did her own children.

"Please," Dawn whispered, she indicated for Goody to bring her ear to her mouth and she whispered something to Goody that I couldn't hear.

They started to do some tests with medical instruments, which they both had a difficult time reading in the dimness of the lanterns.

"Suzannah," Dr. Maars said. "Go get some water. I want you to light a fire too, so we can boil the rags."

I took the bucket that we had brought from the

infirmary and went out to the water pump. It was a relief to be away from that smell, from the dead eyes, how angry they looked… I pumped away and got some of the water out. I was shaking so hard, it kept on sloshing out and having to go back to the pump.

"Let me help you," said a dry voice. I saw one of the whores coming down the steps. I recognized her as one of the girls who had aged out right as I got into the Handmaiden House. Her name had been Tessa. I backed away and let her pump the water. Yes, we were pretty lean in this commune, but not as gaunt and frightening-looking as these girls. She got the bucket filled. "I know you're not supposed to talk to me now."

I didn't speak.

"The Maarses just pronounced the baby as dead inside her. There's no heartbeat, no movement, Dawn has an infection and a fever…" she continued. She studied me for a reaction. "We heard about what you did. I'm surprised you haven't joined us, yet."

I pressed my lips together.

"Come on," she said, picking up the bucket. She assisted me with starting a fire in the pit to put water into the pot. I put the rags in my lap and waited for the water to boil. "This is what life is like here." I looked around; separated, alone, I doubt they got much food, considering how thin they were. I thought about passing out in the laundry from lack of water and food when I had been punished. I wondered how these girls did it.

"Maybe it's best that you don't talk to me."

I gripped the rags in my hands and twisted. The fire crackled. "They think I'm unclean anyway," I muttered.

"Unclean," she snorted humorlessly. "I am convinced that nothing in this world is as unclean as this place. I don't know what I did wrong to end up here." She sat a few feet away from me. "I don't know how I tempt the militia every day when I'm shoveling cow and horse droppings. But they come, every night. All of 'em."

I heard myself cry out in shock; did Silas come here? Did he do something like this to these girls?

"The Maars boy doesn't. That's why they call him queer," she continued. "If he doesn't soon, he's gonna be stoned anyway. They don't send the queer ones here. They just kill 'em. Damned if he does, and damned if he don't."

I blinked. "What does it mean to be queer?" I asked quietly.

"What they do to us… a pair of queers do to each other," she said after a long silence. "Two men together. Or two women. That's forbidden. Once Deacon finds out… he's gone."

I felt sick again.

"Silas did come here. A coupla times, but only to help his parents. They're the last good people in this commune."

We listened to the fire crackle and I smelled the animal defecation on her. How did she live like this?

"The Maarses call us by the names we were born with. Everyone else just calls us 'whore.'"

I shivered.

"Suzannah?" Dr. Maars came out of the tent. "Have you boiled the rags, yet?"

"We're trying," I said. "The water's not boiling."

"We need the rags," he said. "It can't wait."

I stood up and handed him the bucket. "Here."

He ran back into the tent with the rags. I went back in, too, leaving the girl by the fire.

Inside, I saw the other girls had backed away, and Goody Maars was taking the rags. Dawn's pants had been removed, and I could see the underside of her belly; slightly stretched out, but not as large as most expecting wives got in the commune. She was holding her legs together tightly.

"I know this is going to hurt, Dawn," Goody said, dumping alcohol all over her hands, lathering them. "But your baby is dead. We can try to save you, but we have to get the baby out." Dawn began to whimper. "Be strong. Emily, can you hold Dawn's hand? Ephraim, get the other."

"No!" Dawn sobbed.

"We have to try to save your life," Goody Maars pleaded.

"Dawn, you still have worth," Dr. Maars said. "And value. Let us try to save you…"

"No!" Dawn sobbed. "I don't!"

"Ephraim, hold her other hand," Goody Maars ordered, looking as sick as I felt. "Emily?" The girl who used to be named Emily took Dawn's other hand. "Hold her down. I'm sorry Dawn, I have to try to save you."

"Hell can't be any worse than this!" Dawn cried, going slack.

"Yes, it can be," Goody said. "I live it every day that another girl gets sent here. I'm sorry, I have to do this." She took her hands and I watched Goody do something I never wanted to see again; she parted Dawn's legs, despite her screaming, and then pushed her hand inside the girl. I then understood why I had been banned from my mother's births and why they kept the secrets of virginity from us girls in the commune.

I ran outside and vomited beside the steps.

I threw up until there was nothing left in my stomach, then heaved several more times, bringing up nothing but bile. At last Dawn stopped screaming. An eerie silence settled over the camp, but I couldn't bear to go back in. The door to the hut opened, and Goody Maars stumbled out, holding her hands before her. Dr. Maars followed. He laid a hand on her shoulder, then led her to the pump.

"What happened?" I asked. "What happened to…Dawn?"

Dr. Maars pumped water over Goody's hands, and she scrubbed them until they were free of blood. "She's dead," he muttered.

"Dead?" Tears leaked down my cheeks.

Sobs wracked Goody's body. "I tried," she wept. "I tried to save that poor girl, but…" She collapsed into her husband's arms.

"There was nothing you could do. Nothing anyone could have done. The infection was too advanced," Dr. Maars said.

"But we *should* be able to do something!" Goody seethed, her anger overpowering her grief. "It's this *place*, Ephraim. Merciful Stars!" She pounded a fist against the pump. "They're going to dump her body in the mass grave. She was a *person*! Just like that baby was a *person*, and they are going to throw her away, like she was a piece of trash. And they do it every, single, *time!*"

Dr. Maars held her close. "Shh."

They stood that way, together, for a few moments more. I felt so ashamed. Goody needed me, and I had run away. I should have stayed. I should have waited and watched. But I was afraid. I had been a coward tonight. I wiped away the tears that were falling down my cheeks.

"That girl didn't want to live," I whispered.

"That *girl* was a *person*. With a name," Dr. Maars interrupted me, more harshly than I think he intended. Then more kindly, "Her name was Dawn. The only thing we can do for her now is honor her memory. We need to remember her name."

"But we're not supposed to," I uttered. "Deacon says…"

"Deacon is a liar!" Dr. Maars shouted.

His voice echoed across the field, startling a flock of birds to burst into flight. As his words faded into the night Dr. Maars continued in a low voice. "Deacon is a liar. He is not to be trusted. He does this – *this abomination* - to keep in control. He orders the militia to come in here and rape these girls. They hold them down, beat them, and then take them, like a pack of wild dogs.

"These girls aren't the sinners. They're victims. The real sinners are the Elders who encourage this and Deacon who organized it. He is a corruption! He destroys whatever, or whoever, stands in his way. Why do you think he's worked so hard convinced you and the other women in this commune that you are evil and that you're too stupid to think for yourself? You are none of those things. You are *not* evil until you *choose* evil.

"Suzannah, listen to me," he commanded. "You have done nothing wrong. Your purity is intact. But even if your purity was compromised, that would not make you, or any other woman in this commune, any less important. Nobody deserves to be treated like *this*. No one deserves to die alone and be forgotten. No one is disposable."

CHAPTER 9

I was shaken. Horrified. And a number of other things.

This is what happened to the girls when they aged out or did something with a boy? I wasn't sure if the Maarses were right or not. How could Deacon be wrong? He had to be wrong; these girls did not deserve what he was allowing the men of the commune to do to them.

I walked back with Dr. Maars and Goody to the main building knowing that every time I closed my eyes, I'd see Dawn, held down, screaming. The realization of what virginity actually was hit me. I was still a virgin, although I was scared of everything, now; scared of my purity being taken, of what I had learned, what was going to happen, if I could protect it or not…

"How do I ever trust Deacon again?" I whispered.

"You don't," Goody said, wiping her eyes. "You must know that deep down, he doesn't have your best interests at heart, only his own."

We walked a little further. "Why did you take me there?" I asked quietly.

"I wanted you to understand," Goody said.

"Why we're different. Silas has accompanied us before, and that why he doesn't go. And this why you

87

shouldn't trust Deacon. I wanted you to see the Hard Labor camp first hand and understand what it really is. The religion he's forcing us to follow, it's not real. It's twisted, contrived — far from the true religion it was based on. He had the original religion's holy book, but won't let anybody read it, because he's afraid it will challenge his authority. What he's doing to us, manipulating us, is only for his own benefit. Nobody is capable of speaking out because they're so controlled they don't know how."

"Did you think you'd kill Dawn?" I asked.

Goody shook her head. "I've performed the procedure to get a dead baby out of the mother hundreds of times before, 'stripping the membranes' as it's called, but the sac containing the baby was infected. She was so infected, it was in her blood, going towards her heart, and there was blood between her guts... I couldn't save her."

"I honestly thought we'd be able to," Dr. Maars said. "Deacon doesn't want those girls back in our infirmary. Had we been able to take her to the infirmary, we'd have had a different outcome."

"What if I end up there?" I asked quietly. "In the camp, alone, impure..."

"We will take you away from here," Goody Maars said firmly.

"We can't take everyone, Marissa," Dr. Maars said. "We don't have the room."

"We will take Suzannah away from there," Goody Maars said. "She knows, now."

"There's nothing out there," I said, "for you to take me to. The Teeth will get us or the reanimated dead."

"You don't know that," Dr. Maars said. "All you know is what Deacon's told you."

"All that's out there is The Ruins," I said. "Silas says you've taken him."

They exchanged a glance. "You know about The Ruins?" Dr. Maars asked.

I nodded.

"Keep that a secret," Dr. Maars said. "But there's much more out there than the Ruins. One day, we'll take you, when it's safe. But for now, go back to the Handmaiden House and go to bed."

My life continued as if Dawn had never died. Deacon never mentioned her, he never even mentioned that a hard labor whore was dead as if she didn't matter. I saw her mother, who had been a third wife of one of the oldest Elders: she didn't seem to care. I wondered if she even considered that she had a daughter at all once she had been stripped of her name and virginity. Like my parents did to me, now.

I remembered what Dr. and Goody Maars had impressed upon me; the girl's life was important. We had to honor her memory by remembering her name. Nobody else would. My heart ached when I thought of her; how scared she had been, how close to death, but wanting to die. Instead, life went on like nothing had happened. But I knew something had happened, and I was changed inside.

As I was laying in bed a few nights later, trying to go to sleep, I thought about how that girl, the one that had been named Tessa, had said about Silas. Silas didn't come to unify with these girls against their wills. They thought he was queer, and I understood now why that name hurt him so much when I called him that.

The days continued and the weather became warmer. I continued to clean Silas's room and cook for him. Dr. Maars read stories and I stopped to listen to him. I usually missed out on folding Silas's laundry, so I usually did it when I arrived back in their quarters. A week after Dawn's death, when Dr. and Goodwife Maars took Telly and Noah to get ready for bed, I went to Silas's room to gather the laundry. I needed to stop listening to the book, start folding his clothes before I left the laundry, and get back to cleaning for Silas, so I decided to say the daily prayers instead to keep myself focused.

"Why do you say those prayers?" Silas asked.

"That's what we're supposed to do," I said, aghast. I turned around and saw him in the doorway.

"Why?"

I realized I didn't know why I said these prayers.

"I think you can be a good person without saying them," Silas said.

"But we'd be lost without them. Don't you say them?"

"I say them on my own. In private. I don't do it for all to see."

"The Master wouldn't like that."

"The Master knows what's in my heart. That's all that counts."

"But... you have to say them out loud so everybody knows that you believe them," I said. "If you don't, they'll question if you believe it at all."

"They only make us say them so they can isolate people that don't think like they do. I think you can say the prayers in your head and it be just as important to the Master as it can be to speak it out loud in front of everyone."

"But if everyone thinks you don't believe..."

"What does that matter if they think that? People

think a lot of things about me that aren't true."

I swallowed. I felt a deep sense of shame. "Silas, I'm sorry I said you were queer."

His face went blank. "You know what it means, now?"

"I found out in the hard labor camp. I don't understand why one set of standards holds for the girls and not the boys."

"I don't understand, either."

"Why don't you ask?"

"I have. It got me in trouble."

"Oh… I'm sorry."

"It's alright. I learned not ask questions. If I do, they know I think differently. Not asking questions makes them think I'm not so different."

I picked up the laundry sack. "I'll see you tomorrow."

"Good night."

I went out to the main quarters.

"Suzannah?" Dr. Maars was combing Telly's wet hair out.

"Can she spend the night?" Telly asked.

"I'm just leaving," I said. "Can I take any of your laundry for you?"

"Did Silas say something?"

I swallowed, lowered my eyes and lied. "No, sir."

"Suzannah, we trust you to be a part of our family. We've decided when the coast is clear, we'll take you to the Ruins."

I glanced up and met his eyes. "They're real?"

"Of course they're real," he said.

"What about the reanimated dead?" I asked. "The Teeth?"

He chuckled. "Don't worry about them," he said. "We'll pick a night where we'll be safe from them. Can you keep it a secret?"

I nodded eagerly.

What a great adventure. The Ruins. Kind of like Jim Hawkins, going out to sea on the *Hispaniola*.

"Suzannah, before you leave, there's a box on the table by the door."

"This one?" I asked, seeing a small wooden box sitting on the table.

"Yes. That's for you."

I picked it up cautiously.

"Keep it a secret," he said. "Take it back to the Handmaiden House, but keep that a secret, too."

I nodded, putting it into the laundry sack. "You can trust me."

Life in the commune continued as if Dawn had never died. Deacon never mentioned her. No one even mentioned that a hard labor whore had died. She simply didn't matter.

I saw Dawn's mother at worship. She was the third wife of one of our oldest Elders. If she cared that her daughter had died, she didn't show it. I wondered if she even considered that she had a daughter at all, once she was stripped of her name and virginity.

I wondered if my parents considered me to be dead already. But I considered. Goody Maars had impressed upon me the importance of every life, even Dawn's. I determined to honor her memory by remembering her name. I was convinced that nobody else, other than the Maars family, would.

Yes, life went on like nothing had happened. But something *had* happened.

And I was changed inside because of it.

Laying in bed a few nights later, I thought about Tessa, and what she said about Silas, that he didn't come to unify with the girls against their wills. She thought he was queer. Now I understood why it hurt him so badly when I called him that. I determined I would work harder to control my tongue.

I continued to clean Silas's room and cook for him. I had stopped seeing it as a punishment, and instead looked forward to my time with the Maars family. I loved listening when Dr. Maars read from novels, but it did get in the way of my work, and I wanted to prove at least to myself, that I could be a good wife someday.

One evening while folding Silas's clothes, I decided to focus my thoughts on my work, instead of listening to the stories. To keep my mind occupied, I recited the daily prayers. I didn't realize Silas was standing in the doorway, listening to me.

"Why do you say those prayers," he asked.

I jumped at the sound of his voice.

"That's what we're supposed to do, isn't it?"

"Why?"

I thought about it for a moment, then realized I didn't know why I repeated the prayers.

"I suppose because the Great Master commands it. We'd be lost without them," I finally answered. "Don't you say them?"

"The Great Master knows what's in my heart. That's all that counts."

"But you have to say them out loud so everybody knows that you believe them," I said.

"Can't you say something out loud that you don't believe?"

"But if everyone thinks you don't believe…"

"What does it matter what people think? People think

a lot of things about me that aren't true. What is important is what the Great Master knows."

I swallowed. I felt a deep sense of shame. "Silas, I'm sorry I called you queer."

His face went blank. "You know what it means, now?"

I nodded. "I found out in the hard labor camp." He just stared at me. I picked up the laundry sack. "I'll see you tomorrow."

"Good night."

I pushed past him and headed toward the front door. I passed Dr. Maars combing out Telly's wet hair.

"I'm leaving now," I said. "Can I take any of your laundry for you?"

Dr. Maars ignored my question. Instead he told Telly to go to her mother to finish getting ready for bed. Once she was out of the room he turned his attention to me.

"Suzannah, would you like to go with us to the Ruins?"

My eyes grew wide. "They're real?"

"Of course they're real," he chuckled. "But I need for you to keep it a secret."

I nodded eagerly.

What a great adventure. The Ruins! Like Jim Hawkins, going out to sea on the Hispaniola.

CHAPTER 10

I listened to Dr. Maars read the rest of Treasure Island after going over to pick up Silas and Noah's laundry. I wished so often that this hour could go on forever. I couldn't wait to see the Ruins, too. I didn't dare ask the question of when we'd go. I only trusted that we would someday soon.

Goody delivered a baby one afternoon, and after worship, I sneaked away to see it in the nursery. It was a healthy baby, and it would be allowed to live, even though it was a girl. The baby was so tiny and her little fingers were so soft. Goody had bathed her already, and she was dressed in a diaper and had been wrapped up in a swaddling cloth.

"I can't wait to be a mother," I admitted, admiring her. "What's her name?"

"Samara, I think. She's Danielle's baby, Elder Derrick's second wife," Goody said. "I think she needs her diaper changed, though, if you want to help?"

"Of course."

She took the baby over to the changing area, and carefully set her down on the changing mat, carefully unswaddling her. As Goody unwrapped her, I saw her right arm already had the tracking chip implanted under the back of her wrist, a small scar was sewn up with wire. "They've already implanted her," I noted.

"Yes, Ephraim was called in to do that, but I oversaw it."

"Did it hurt her?" I asked, running the pad of my pinky finger over the little cut. Goody unpinned the diaper and the baby was wet. She wrapped up the cloth carefully and handed it to me.

"Can you put this in the soiled linens, please?"

"Yes, ma'am."

"No, we didn't hurt her when we implanted her. We injected her with some topical numbing agent so she didn't feel anything."

Holding the wet diaper carefully, I put it into the laundry basket. "She's so little! I forget sometimes how small babies are when they're first born."

"She's going to be hungry soon, too. She'll need to nurse; I hope Danielle is awake and ready."

I watched intently as Goody changed her confidently. She had done this a lot in her lifetime, it was obvious. "Do you think I'll be a good mother?" I asked Goody.

I saw the edges of her mouth twitch up. "I think you'll be a wonderful mother, Suzannah. Would you like to carry her back to the bassinet?"

"I'd love to!" I cried, excited at the opportunity to hold Samara as Goody wrapped her up tightly again. Samara was heavy, to my surprise.

"Support her head," Goody instructed. "She doesn't have any neck muscles to hold her head up, yet." Samara's little mouth met my bare collar bone, making me giggle. "She's searching for a nipple, she's hungry."

At the bassinet, Goody showed me how to place my hand on the back of the baby's head as I leaned her forward.

"…And lay her down like this."

"Does she need a blanket?"

"She's swaddled right now, no. She'll be eating soon when we bring Danielle down. It's getting late, and you need to get to our quarters to clean."

"Bye, Samara!" I called, leaning down to kiss her little forehead.

As I gathered Silas and Noah's laundry, I heard a click behind me. I whirled around to see Silas standing there with a satchel in hand the door shut.

"Silas, no! Open the door!" I cried.

"I'm not going to do anything," Silas said. "Except give you this."

He reached into the satchel and produced a book entitled *Jane Eyre*. "Well, not give it to you, but Papa can read this next. It's one of Mother's favorites."

"What's it about?"

"A girl who grows up to be equal with her husband," he said.

"Like your mother?" I whispered.

He nodded.

"It's kind of… dangerous then, isn't it?"

He nodded again. "Yeah. This is one of the books that Deacon doesn't want everybody knowing about. I borrowed another book." He got out another book and showed it to me. I opened it to see the handwriting in it. It was hand-made. "It's a book by a Deacon from years past."

"Oh," I said, disappointed, but I read a line.

"He was a scholar on the holy book. There used to be lots of scholars on the holy book. And lots of holy books."

"Deacon said they were all destroyed by the Teeth's Jihad."

"He doesn't want us reading it. Then, we'll get ideas for ourselves."

I examined the cover; it said, *St. Anathios Holy Orthodox Christian Church* in gold letters against the faded, black leather with curling edges. The words on the inside looked like squiggles until I realized it was writing.

"How do you read this?" I asked.

"It's cursive writing," Silas explained. "We sort of lost it in the commune. Papa still knows how to write in cursive, though. He taught me."

"What's it about?"

"It's a journal, actually. This holy man lived around here before the war."

"You mean when we were flooded?"

"No, there was... He's really smart... listen..." He flipped the pages and found something. "*...If the Bible were completely lost, we could rewrite it with love.*" He flipped a few more pages. "*There's something special about motherhood that a man will never understand. The mother and baby have a special bond a man will never experience. Maybe women can't be ministers, but they have an important role. We are all important and indisposable in the body of Christ... Role does not equal rank, all roles are important in the church.*"

"What's he talking about?" I whispered.

"He saw the Holy Book very, very differently than Deacon does," he said. "He's amazing. He was born in... in... Pen-sla-vania? I think that's how it's said. They called him Father, not Deacon, though. He says that love is more important that the law. He was a priest in a small church a few miles from here, smaller than our chapel. I think the church still stands. I don't know if anybody goes there anymore..."

"Why would we go there?"

"There are a lot more people in this world than just us."

"There are other communes?"

He nodded. "And cities. And towns. Billions and billions of people."

"Past the Ruins?"

He nodded.

"I want to go," I whispered.

"I'll take you. Tomorrow night, I promise."

I took the laundry sack and started down the hall to the exit. A group of Elders were coming down the hallway, and discussing something. I stopped along the wall, and lowered the laundry sack, keeping my eyes down until they passed.

"… The latest crop is looking very puny. Are those girls even breeding stock?"

I was tempted to look up. But I kept my head down.

"Fewer and fewer children are being born. We'll run into problem soon."

One of the Elders stopped in front of me, and slipped his fingers under my chin, and lifted my face. I looked into his eyes for a moment and diverted away. He examined my face and turned my face to profile. He studied me. I felt a tingly sensation of dread in the pit of my stomach. I knew his name: Morris. I didn't know he was a full Elder yet.

"Very nice," he murmured and let go of my chin.

He caught up with the rest of the Elders.

Breathing a sigh of relief, I watched as they went on down the hall towards their own quarters. I picked up my laundry sack and took a deep breath, going towards the exit to the courtyard.

That evening, I was giddy with excitement. Silas is going to take me away from the commune! My hands trembled as I served Silas his dinner. He grinned at me and I returned it. It was our secret. A thought crossed my mind.

I wonder if Goody and the Doctor know. Will they go with us?

The thought was driven away by the piercing shriek of the commune alarm. The reanimated dead were back! Or it might be the Teeth. We had to get to the shelters. I gathered Telly into my arms and started towards the basement. I bit my lip in concern. I felt anxious, not for myself, but for the girls in the hard labor camp. They had no basement shelter for protection. Odd to think that a year ago I would not have cared what happened to them; they were the lowest of the low, despised and rejected by the Great Master.

They were human to me now. And I was powerless to help them.

"Look for the Elders," Silas whispered in my ear.

I shot him a questioning glance.

"Every time the alarm sounds, when Teeth come back, they disappear."

I looked around crowded basement shelter. Women panicking, children crying, men huddled against the walls, everyone terrified. Silas nodded to me once more, then joined the other militia boys as they rushed against the throng toward the weapon storehouse.

I around the room. Even in the dim light, I realized Silas was right. I didn't see a single Elder.

Two militia boys began pulling the heavy doors closed when someone shouted, "Wait!"

Goody and Dr. Maars squeeze through just in time, carrying their bags of medications with them. The doors closed behind them, and the militia boys dropped a thick crossbar into the iron fitting. Goody went from family to family, speaking quiet words of encouragement while the doctor administered medications to those who were overcome by fear. One older man clutched his chest, and his legs shook. Dr. Maars gave him an injection of something, and the man seemed to just go to sleep, but he was breathing easily again.

Before long everyone stopped talking, and the only sound remaining was the quite snuffling of children, the collective breathing of everyone in the shelter, and the sound of ours beating in our ears. I held Telly close, as I recalled the events surrounding previous attacks from the outside.

The alarm sounded when one of the reanimated dead got inside the protective walls. Our militia boys were always able to dispatch them quickly. By the time the 'all clear' bell was sounded, the bodies were always already on a pyre, burning.

It was necessary, the Elders told us, to burn the bodies as soon as possible. Otherwise, the virus that had infected these dead bodies might spread throughout the commune. It made sense, I supposed. But I began to wonder if it was true.

The mood in the shelter shifted from stark panic to resignation. We never know how long it would take before the Elders deemed it safe to come out. I settled into a more comfortable spot on the floor, and sing soft songs to Telly to keep her from being frightened. But if the child in my lap was scared, she didn't show it.

After a while, Goody found us and sat down beside me. She was exhausted. In the dim light, I could see Dr. Maars continuing to move among the people, treating any who needed help or encouragement.

"He won't stop," Goody said, a look of loving admiration shining from her eyes. "As long as someone needs him, he will not stop."

"Are you feeling alright," I asked.

"I'm trying to stay calm and help where I can. This is an emergency, right?"

"Yes, it is," I agreed.

"No, it's not," Telly whispered loudly.

"Shh," Goody hissed, stroking her hair.

"But, I'm not scared," Telly replied.

I suddenly realized I wasn't scared, either. I could find nothing to be afraid of.

She rubbed Telly's back and gave me a knowing look. "Don't show it," she whispered.

I wasn't sure how to acted scared when I wasn't. I felt like that would be lying.

We sat in the drowsy silence. The room was close and still, and it seemed as if we were all sedated.

"How much longer?" Telly asked.

"You never know," Goody tried to comfort her. "The longest I've ever been down here was twenty-four hours."

"Twenty-four hours?" Telly gasped. "A whole day?"

"It happened long before either of you were born," Goody said. Then she added, "It's wasn't so bad, but I was very hungry when we got out."

"I wish we could read in here," Telly said.

"Shh!" Goody whispered, pressing a hand over Telly's mouth. Although she hadn't said it too loudly, a few people looked in our direction. I was grateful that most of them were under the effects of the medicine, and would likely not remember Telly's comment.

"Sorry," Telly whispered.

"Why don't you go play with the other girls in your class?" Goody suggested.

"I want to stay here with Suzannah."

I squeezed her in a hug.

There was a sudden thump above our heads and the people gasped collectively. I wasn't scared. I actually wanted to see a reanimated corpse. I wanted to see this creature that was banging on the walls, face-to-face. I wanted to see the decomposed body walking around, to prove that it was real. I wanted to know if all the things I had been taught my entire life were true? Or if I had believed a lie.

A wordless-yell came from the tiny window at the top of the stairs, and a hand slapped across the dirty window. Every eye strained to see through the cloudy window, and every person in the room backed away from it.

Except for me. I didn't move. Then I realized I had to act afraid. I couldn't afford to stand out. I moved with the crowd against the opposite wall, holding Telly. The figure outside yelped and gibbered, making inhuman sounds that weren't recognizable as words. I wished I could see him.

I wondered where the Elders and Deacon were. Deacon is too old to fight. He told us so. *So, why is he out there, hunting our enemies? Shouldn't he be in here, with us?*

I saw my mother holding my younger brothers. She saw me, and I could see disgust overpower her fear, if only for a moment. Oddly, I didn't feel sad. Instead, I pulled Telly more tightly into my arms and enjoyed seeing the frown of disapproval that creased her face.

Let her be ashamed of me, I thought.

A burst of gunshots rang out from the other side of the door. Screams echoed off the walls inside the shelter. There were shouts and the sound of running feet. There appeared to be fighting outside the window. A hand clawed at the glass, then blood dripped down and the hand fell away.

"It's over," Goody whispered.

I lowered Telly to the floor but held her hand tightly.

"I want to see," I said to Goody. I crossed to the dirty, blood spattered window and peered out. A figure wearing militia greens was gesturing with his hands to someone I couldn't see. I could hear the men talking, but couldn't understand their words.

Then I saw it; the corpse of the reanimated dead.

Only he wasn't dead. *That's one of the boys from the militia. I can't tell which one, but I know I've seen him before!*

I felt anger boiling up in my gut, but I remembered Goody told me to act scared. No sense getting myself burned at the stake for unbelief.

"Stars! They killed one of the reanimated dead. We're safe," I cried out. It was a lie. I knew it was a lie. Somehow, I felt the Great Master would forgive me for it.

Oakley pressed a hand to her heart and giggled with relief. "We're safe!" she wept and laughed at the same time. "Oh, the Great Master loves us. Master bless our militia for keeping us safe when we couldn't protect ourselves."

There was such communal cheering, clapping, and goodwill that for a brief moment I thought they might welcome me back into the fold. I was wrong. I reached to embrace Oakley when Simber stepped between us. The look on her face told me I was not welcome.

"We haven't been released, yet," a voice from the back of the room called out. "There could be more of those unholy creatures roaming about the commune. Let's settle down, shall we?"

I returned to my place beside Goody Maars, and Telly immediately reclaimed her place in my lap.

I was angry. Beyond angry. *We had been tricked. How many times had this same scene played out? And why go to all the trouble. Did they just want to keep us from exploring beyond the borders of the commune?*

Did the reanimated dead still exist? Had they ever existed?

Were the Teeth still out there, eating human flesh? What human flesh? We were all inside the commune. If Deacon and the Elders were to be believed there weren't any other people for them to eat. Had they starved to death, or found something else to feed on?

The longer I pondered it, the angrier I grew. Deacon was a liar! It was a traitorous thought, but I didn't care.

The red emergency lights flashed off, replaced by the normal white lights. We could see clearly again. The intercom buzzed, and a voice announced, "We killed it. It will take a few moments to clean up the contaminated blood. We don't want anyone getting the fever."

You could feel the tension in the room dissipate. I felt everyone in the shelter relax. It was almost visible. All around the room people closed their eyes and slept. I didn't sleep. I didn't want to. I just wanted to be away from these people and their blind obedience.

It was another hour before we were finally given the all clear bell. The two militia guards unbarred the door and pushed it open. The sun was rising over the horizon and the stench of bleach burning flesh stung my sinuses, almost making me gag.

The youngest members of the militia, 13-year-old boys, were scrubbing the walls with pink rags.

"It bled a lot," I heard one Elder saying to another. "Thank the Great Master there was only one. The pyre's already burning."

I carried Telly up the stairs as quickly as I could. "Where are we going, Suzannah?" Telly asked.

"To the pyre," I said. "I want to see something."

A group of militia soldiers stood guard around the pyre, preventing the curious from getting too close.

"Don't go any closer!" Telly begged.

"Are you scared?" I asked.

"Yes! I don't want to see."

"Stay here. I'll come back for you." I set her down beside the tree and worked my way through the gathering crowd to the blazing bonfire.

"Suzannah," a voice from the militia called out. It was Silas, in his militia uniform, armed with a rifle. "Suzannah, don't!"

"I want to see it," I said through clenched teeth. "I need to see it."

"You shouldn't." His eyes begged me to relent. I just shook my head. I had to see it. I had to know.

Silas took my hand and elbowed his way through the crowd, close enough for me to feel the searing heat of the inferno; close enough to see the figure on the burning pyre.

It was a human body. Its hair was burnt off and its skin was black and blistered from the flames, but it was definitely human. And it was definitely not a man. As the flames licked up the wood to consume the body, I recognized the face; it was Tessa from the Hard Labor camp.

I opened my mouth to scream, but no words would come out. Someone grabbed my arm and jerked me backward. I fell to the ground at the feet of Elder Morris, his face twisted with rage. He bent low and slapped me hard across the face. Through my pain, I saw him unbuckle his belt. I panicked and raised my arm in front of my face as he whipped his belt out of the belt loops of his trousers and slapped down. The leather bit into my arm, sending shockwaves of pain throughout my body.

"This is for being where you should not be," he growled.

I gasped for air. I rolled onto my stomach and clawed at the ground, trying to crawl away from the blows. A hand grabbed my hair and pulled my head back. I thought my neck would snap.

I heard a smack and a grunt, and then suddenly, silence. I rolled to my back and saw Silas standing over the unconscious body of Elder Morris. Silas was breathing heavily, clenching and unclenching his fists. Morris moaned and opened his eyes. Silas dropped to his knees, grabbed a handful of the Elder's hair with his left hand, lifted his head, then balled his right hand into a fist and thrust it into his face.

There was a sickening crack. I wasn't sure if it came from Morris's face or Silas's hand. Morris lay still, like a heavy sack of potatoes.

"Don't you ever touch her again!" Silas shouted.

The militiamen, who had stood stunned during the altercation, finally regained their wits and grabbed Silas and me.

"Take them to Deacon," the commander of the group said. "Let him decide their punishment."

✦✦✦

The militia tied Silas's hands behind his back. I suppose they didn't see me as much of a threat because the left my arms free. Still, I was escorted by two of the young men; one gripped my left arm, the other my right.

The one on my right leaned in close and breathed into my ear, "I can't wait to take you."

"Don't touch me!" I cried.

He grinned, walked in front of me and stopped. The grin never left his face as he casually backhanded me across the face. Then he reached out and grabbed my breast.

"Once your hair is cut, I'll touch you however I want," he whispered in my ear. He resumed his position to my right, and together the two militia boys dragged me to Deacon's office. Silas was already there, forced to his knees before Deacon's massive desk. The one on my right shoved me forward, and I fell flat on the floor beside Silas.

"Leave them here," Sub-Elder Thomas said. He sat for a moment in a small chair beside Deacon's desk, studying us, as if we were a scientific specimen of great interest, something he had never seen before. My heart pounded. Silas met his stare with bold defiance but said nothing.

"Deacon is on his way," Thomas said at last. The Sub-Elder then rose, crossed the room and left, closing the door behind him without another word.

"I didn't realize I was doing anything wrong," I snuffled. My anger-birthed bravery was washing away by the reality of our situation. "I just wanted to look at the pyre." Tears started to form at the corners of my eyes.

"I did," Silas said. "I knew it was forbidden for a woman to look." He turned to me, and I could see his face swelling, where the militia boys had obviously beaten him. "I couldn't stand watching that… animal… laying his hands on you." He smiled at me, and my heart swelled. "I'll take full responsibility. It wasn't your fault."

"You can't do that," I whispered.

"Yes, I can," Silas said. "Expect me to just sit back and watch while that bully beats you like a common thief? No. I won't stand for it."

"But I was doing something wrong."

"No, you weren't. The bonfires after an attack are to show the people that we are destroying the body. They want people to see it."

"It was Tessa's body," I whispered.

"Shh," Silas warned. He looked around the room, then mouthed. "He's listening." Aloud he said, "No, you're mistaken. The body was one of the reanimated dead. It breached the perimeter and was heading for the basement because it smelled all of you. It was hungry. We killed it, but we had to fully destroy the body before it infected the whole community."

Silas stared at me, his eyes pleading with me to agree with his version of events.

The door opened and Deacon strode in with Sub-Elder Thomas trailing behind, like a puppy at its master's heels. Silas and I both stood and bowed our heads.

"Suzannah Commons, in my office. Again," he sighed. "I must say I'm not surprised. I had hoped your punishment was sufficient to keep you on the straight and narrow. And Silas Maars. When I was told there was an altercation at the pyre, I didn't expect you to be involved.

"What to do with you two? That's the question, isn't it." Deacon crossed behind his desk and sat in his polished leather chair, which gave an ominous creak under his weight. He drummed his fingers on the thick oak desktop as he pondered. At last, he said, "I have been told that you two have contrived to form something of a friendship. I know this cannot be, for inherent in every friendship is a certain sense of equality that exists between the two parties."

He fixed me with a stare. "Let me be perfectly clear, Suzannah; you are not equal to Silas, nor to any other man in this community. You are a female. You were created to serve. You are unintelligent; you are incompetent; and quite frankly, my dear, you aren't even all that pretty. You rarely accomplish all of your regular tasks, and typically leave your punishment work half-finished. Silas does most of it for you, isn't that so?"

I felt my cheeks burn. I could not meet his gaze. He turned his attention to Silas.

"Silas, you are, by all accounts, a fine young man from a well-respected family. You have acquitted yourself honorably in the militia. Still, I have no reports of you taking advantage of your… recreational prerogatives… in the hard labor camp. As such I am not pleased to find you here. You must understand that with all the dangers that surround our community, maintaining order is paramount. While men can be reasoned with, children and women must be controlled by the appropriate application of the rod.

"Tell me, Silas," Deacon reasoned. "If a man's wife does something wrong, even out of ignorance, does she not deserve a beating for it?"

Silas pressed his lips together. I could tell he was fighting back the anger that was seething behind his eyes. He took a deep breath and met Deacon's gaze.

"Sir, isn't the husband responsible for determining

whether his wife's offense warrants a beating?"

"Don't debate with me, boy," Deacon snapped. "Answer the question. Yes or no?"

"With respect, Sir. If I allow my wife to do something worthy of a beating, isn't that my fault?"

Silas stood erect, his shoulders back, his gaze steady.

"I'm ready to assume full responsibility. After all, as the Great Master teaches; a man is his wife's keeper."

Deacon slammed his hand down on his desk.

"But you are not Suzannah's husband," Deacon shouted. "Nor will you ever be."

Deacon took a moment to regain his composure. He sighed, as if frustrated by dealing with a petulant child. At last, he pulled open the bottom drawer of his desk, reached in and drew out a coiled whip.

"I'll take the punishment," Silas blurted out.

"Suzannah did nothing wrong!"

"Ah, but she did," Deacon said, his voice rich and resonate, like when he preached a sermon. "Curiosity is a sin." He shook out the coils of the long, black whip, and dragged the length of it across his palm. "Especially in girls."

"Let me tell you a story about curiosity, Suzannah." He looked at me and smiled. "You know how curious cats are? Well, one day a barn cat came across a spider. Curious, the cat tapped the spider with its paw. The spider tried to run away, but every time it moved, the cat was there, reaching out, tapping it, playing with it. The cat was curious, you see. At last the cat put its paw down on the spider.

"Can you guess what happened next, Suzannah?"

I shook my head.

I had a dreadful feeling in the pit of my stomach.

"The spider bit the cat's paw," the smile never left

Deacon's face. "It turns out this spider was a black widow; quite poisonous. The venom from the spider's bite coursed through the cat's veins, until at last, it reached its heart. The cat died, a horrible, painful death. And the sad thing is, nobody cared. You see, everyone knew it was the cat's own fault. If the cat hadn't been so curious, it would not have gotten bitten. You see, Suzannah, curiosity killed the cat.

"This is the nature of sin. You obtained forbidden knowledge. Forbidden knowledge results in the loss of purity. The loss of purity is sin, and when sin conceives, it brings forth death. Then, what good are you? Like the impure girls to are sent to the hard labor camp, you are good for nothing, except to be cast out and trodden under the foot of men."

There was no smile on Deacon's face now. It had been replaced by the vicious snarl of an indignant judge. A quick flick of his wrist and the whip flew out to its full length, cracking the air a few inches from my face.

I swallowed, shaking, staring at the floor, not daring to move. My anger evaporated into fear. Dark, abject fear. Deacon pulled the whip back, doubling it as I had seen my father do with his belt when he punished my mother for an infraction.

"Suzannah, lift up your skirt. Bend over, and place your palms on the desk."

I was too frightened to move, so I just stood there. Deacon pursed his lips, stood and walked behind me. I felt his hand between my shoulder blade, and gasped in surprise as he shoved me forward.

To keep from falling I grabbed the edge of his desk. I felt my skirt being raised and flung over my back, then the sharp, breathtaking pain of the whip slapping across the backs of my thighs.

I tried to cry out, but no sound would come. The whip struck my thighs again. I thought my legs would collapse from the pain. Once more the whip cracked, and at last, a wail burst from my lips. I cried. I begged for him to stop. Hot tears flowed down my cheeks. Two more blows followed. Then they stopped, and I did collapse to the floor, weeping and quivering, in pain and shame. Silas and Sub-Elder Thomas had seen my legs!

"I've had to do this to women much older than you," I heard Deacon say, as he walked back to his desk. He sat down again, and as if I was no longer worthy of his attention, addressed Silas.

"This is how you train up your wife in the way she should go, Silas," he said. "If you are wise, you will learn from it, and apply this lesson once you are married. You may return to your quarters. I'll send word to your sergeant. I'm sure he will find some appropriate training to keep you occupied and take your mind off Suzannah. Suzannah, you are to go back to the Handmaiden House and report to the Matron. I suspect she may have something that will help keep your curiosity in check. You're both dismissed."

I regained my feet. I couldn't even raise my eyes to look at Silas as we walked out of Deacon's office, I was so ashamed and embarrassed. The door closed behind us, and we were alone.

"I'm sorry," I whispered. "I am so, so sorry."

"I hate him," Silas whispered, his eyes narrowing to slits. "I hate that man. He's a monster."

"Shh! You mustn't say such things. Not here. Not out loud."

Silas shook his head, but he held his tongue. He took me by the arm and started pulling me along as he walked. "I'm taking you to the infirmary."

"You can't," I protested. "Deacon told me to go to the Handmaiden House."

"Stars, you're injured," Silas seethed. "Deacon said that you are inferior to me, right? That means you have to obey me, and I said you're going to the infirmary! But first, we're going to my parent's quarters."

I nodded. I was confused and in pain. And Deacon was right; I was obviously too ignorant to make my own decisions. I followed Silas to the Maars quarters. Goody Maars was inside knitting by candlelight. When she saw us, she shot to her feet. "Good and merciful stars, where have you been?" she cried. Directing a disapproving gaze at me she added, "What were you thinking, looking into the pyre? And you left Telly alone!"

"Suzannah was lashed," Silas interrupted her.

Goody nodded. "I expected no less. Come. We'll fix you up."

She led me down the hall into the infirmary. A few sick or injured folk lay sleeping in beds against the wall. Ruth, the infirmary matron, sat in a rocking chair, dozing. She looked up as we entered but said nothing as Goody ushered me into an examining room.

"Lift your skirt," she said. I obeyed, allowing her to examine the backs of my thighs. I winced as her cool fingers traced the burning lash wounds.

She sighed in frustration. "Lie face down on the table," she said. "I'll be back in a moment."

I'm not sure how long Goody was gone, but it was the first time since the pyre that I had time to just think. My thoughts drifted over the events of the day, and question formed that demanded answers.

Why was I lashed? When did Tessa die? Why had they burn Tessa's body instead of dumping her? Was that the fate of all the girls in the hard labor camp?

The answers came crashing in on me, although I didn't want to accept it.

Tessa! Poor Tessa. Outcast, abandoned, abused, dying then burned beyond recognition, like so much garbage.

I brushed my hair back from my face and realized tears were leaking down my cheeks.

At last Goody Maars returned holding a glass bottle and a syringe. "I'm going to give you something to numb the pain, Suzannah," she said. "This might sting a little."

She withdrew some of the liquid and then flicked the syringe with her finger a few times. She pressed the plunger, forcing a bit of the fluid to squirt out through the needle. I shivered. I didn't like needles. She pulled my skirt back up to reveal my thighs. "Try not to think about it."

Easy for her to say. I felt the needle piercing my skin. A little sting? I tried not to cry, but the tears came anyway. She repeated the process with my other leg, then pulled my skirt back down. "He hit you hard," she said. "Your legs are still bleeding a bit. You're going to need stitches. Try to rest a bit. I'll be back once the numbing agent takes effect."

I nodded, wiping the tears from my eyes. Goody dimmed the lights and left, closing the door behind her.

I lay in the darkened room, staring at the flashing green dot under my forearm where my microchip was. I couldn't feel the burning sensation in the back of my legs any longer. At last, Goody knocked on the door and came into the room. She flipped on the lights and set a tray down on a counter next to me. She turned on the white noise machine. I assumed she was getting another migraine.

Goody lifted my skirt off my thighs and I heard her handling the tools on the tray. I turned my head to see her threading a needle. She talked as she stitched my wounds.

"When I was a young girl, Ephraim was brought into the infirmary to be trained by my father. He was going to be the commune's next doctor. I remember just looking at him and all the feeling that would rise up inside me. And when he looked at me, I felt hot and cold at the same time; butterflies would dance in my stomach. To my surprise, Ephraim felt the same way about me. Ephraim began bringing me secret gifts, we'd walk together alone when we had a few moments. We became friends. We got into situations like this with Deacon. I was lashed more than once.

"Our feelings were natural, but they were not allowed. This commune is completely unnatural. This commune is all about bending the human will against its nature. They want marriage to be a contract, a source of power and control, not a union based on love. Do you understand what I'm telling you?"

I nodded, but the confused look on my face betrayed me.

"Suzannah, the only reason I wasn't sent to the Hard Labor camp was because my papa was the commune's doctor, and he had significant leverage with Deacon and the Elders. I was allowed to marry Ephraim, but that was a major exception to the way things are usually done here. Things have changed for the worse since those days, and Ephraim doesn't have as much influence on Deacon as my papa had.

"What I'm saying is, you have to avoid his notice as much as possible. If you keep behaving this way, we won't be able to protect you. Do you understand?"

"I wasn't trying to attract any attention, I just wanted to…"

"I know," she cut me off. "You're curious. Silas told me about Deacon and his cat story. Deacon told me the same story when I was your age.

"I want you to listen to me Suzannah. This is important. Curiosity is not a sin. The Great Master created humans to be curious, to gather knowledge. But you have to be wise. Going to the pyre to see the corpse of one of the reanimated dead was a mistake, Suzannah; a serious mistake. The Elders notice such things. And next time the punishment may be worse than a lashing. You could be cast out into the Hard Labor camp."

The truth of Goody's words was starting to sink in, and I shuddered. But my curiosity got the better of me. I had to know. "It wasn't the corpse of the reanimated dead on the pyre, was it?" I asked. "Or one of the Teeth?"

She sighed. "No. There hasn't been an attack on the commune since before I was born. The militia uses a dead body from the labor camp and makes a show of burning it."

"Are they real at all; the reanimated dead?"

She put one more stitch in my leg, then finally answered, "No."

"Silas told me that they weren't a problem. He told me he was going to take me to the Ruins. He promised."

"Silas is showing off for you," she shook her head.

"He wants to impress you."

I was stunned!

Silas wants to impress me?

"Why?"

Goody laughed softly to herself and patted my calf. "Ah, the way of a man with a maid," she whispered. She turned back to me. "Silas is going too far, too fast. He's being foolish. We'll take you there soon, Ephraim and I. But it takes a great deal of planning, and you will never get out of here with your ID chip still activated." She tied off the last stitch. "There. All done."

"You can deactivate your ID chip? How? And how do we get out?" I asked.

"Too many questions for one day," Goody answered. "Trust me. There is a way, but it's a secret. You'll know soon enough."

I tried to ask another question, but I forgot what I wanted to ask. Goody's face started to blur, and I found myself drifting away.

"I gave you something to help you sleep. Close your eyes now," Goody whispered as she stroked my hair.

I nodded and obeyed.

CHAPTER 11

$\mathbf{A}$ loud knock jarred me for my slumber. I opened my eyes, confused and disoriented. *This isn't the Handmaiden House,* I thought. *Where am I?*

The door opened and Ruth, the Infirmary Matron stuck her head through the door. "Get up, girl. It's almost six o'clock."

Memories of the night before came crashing back. *I'm late for the kitchens!* I kicked off the blanket and immediately regretted the sudden movement as the stitched up wound on my thighs screamed at me in protest. I gingerly put on my shoes, took a brief moment to make sure my hair was tucked away in a modest braid, then hurried toward the kitchens.

Women were already bustling around by the time I arrived. I rushed to take my place, hoping no one had noticed my tardiness. My job most mornings was to stir the protein mush constantly so it didn't burn on the bottom. I grabbed a long, wooden spoon, mounted a small stool by the oven and started stirring. Three other women performed the same task.

It was important to keep the mush from burning. For one thing, burnt mush was not suitable for eating and had to be thrown away.

We didn't have enough food to waste. More importantly, at least to me, was that I was also tasked with cleaning the massive cauldron the mush was cooked in. If it burned on the bottom, my job took at least twice as long.

I stood over the stove top, stirring, the backs of my legs throbbing. I could see my reflection in the bottom of a copper skillet that was hanging above the stove with other unused cookware. My cheek, where Elder Morris struck me, was swollen, and a greenish-purple bruise was forming. I touched it. It was still tender. I looked away from my reflection and concentrated on stirring the mush.

Once the meal was prepared, I carried serving bowls to the different tables in the dining hall, covering them with clean dishcloths to keep the flies from the food. I stopped at the Maarses' table and stood with my eyes down, waiting for their arrival. A group of Elders entered the dining hall, speaking to each other in low voices. The skin on the back of my neck crawled. They were talking about Silas. And me. If I could hear them, I knew everyone else in the hall could hear them too. I felt people staring at me.

A hand on my shoulder startled me, but my fear turned to relief when I realized it was Goody. Silas, Noah, and Dr. Maars sat down at the table. Goody and Telly stood on either side of me. As Goody served her husband, Telly tugged on my skirt. I bent down to listen as she whispered in my ear.

"Suzannah! Are you alright?"

"Yes, I am. Thank you," I lied.

"Can I kiss it and make it better?"

"No, Telly. I'm afraid where it hurts, you can't kiss."

She frowned and took my hand.

When it was my turn to serve Silas, I could see the Elders watching us. It was important that I behave myself.

"Are you alright?" he whispered.

"I'm fine," I lied again. I hoped the Great Master would overlook my sin.

Silas didn't look at me, but I could feel the tension rolling off him. I wanted to stroke his shoulder, to make him feel less alone, but they were all watching us.

"We'll talk later," Silas whispered.

I performed my duties at the laundry, being careful to fully complete all my assigned tasks as quickly as possible. I kept my eyes lowered and tried hard to not call attention to myself. At lunchtime, I made my way back to the kitchens to prepare Silas's meal. I was surprised when saw the kitchen matron butchering a lamb carcass. Animals usually weren't culled until the fall. This one must have suffered a broken leg in a fall, and had to be put down.

"Where did this come from," I asked, then bit my tongue. *Your curiosity is going to be the death of you, yet!*

"It was a gift from Deacon. We will have stew tonight, and salt and dry the rest for later in the season when meat is scarce," the kitchen matron said. "Go and work on the marinade, Suzannah."

I tied an apron around my waist and fetched rice and glass jars filled with canned tomatoes from the pantry. I stopped to watch the butchery process and noticed a large hole in animal's side.

"Ouch!" I cried out in pain and raised my hand to my ear. The kitchen matron stood behind me with her fists on her hips.

"Get back to work, or you'll get more than a flick of the ear," she warned me.

"Yes, Matron," I curtsied and hurried about my duties. *Pay attention to what you're doing,* I admonished myself. I went back to chopping vegetables for the stew. I placed the vegetables into the cauldron, then gathered chunks of meat, which we would sear in the cast iron skillets before adding to the stew. I picked up a section of rib, and a small, round piece of metal fell out and rolled across the prep table. I recognized it. Buckshot. This lamb was shot, not slaughtered.

"Was Jane Eyre real?" I asked Goody Maars as she assisted me with changing the sheets in Silas and Noah's room that night. We spent much of the evening reading *Jane Eyre* while making sure I got all my punishment work finished.

I was fascinated by the book; an entire story about a girl and falling in love with a man. Within a few pages, I understood why this was Goody Maars' favorite book. I wanted Dr. Maars to read the whole thing in one night, but that was not possible.

"No. But Charlotte Brontë was," Goody Maars answered.

"Charlotte," I wrinkled my brow. "That is a girl's name, right?"

She nodded.

"A girl wrote a book?"

"Yes," Goody Maars said. "A woman wrote that book."

"But...how? How could a woman write a book? Just think how long it would take. With all the work to do, how could she find the time? Could you write a book?"

"So many questions," Goody laughed. "Yes, I suppose if I wanted to, I could write a book. And I suppose, you could write one too if you felt the need."

I shook my head, a smiled turning up the corners of my mouth. "I could never do anything so wonderful."

"You might be surprised what you can do if you really want to."

"What would I write about?"

"I don't know," Goody said. "Perhaps one day, you'll write a book about Home."

"I don't think Deacon would like that."

"No, I wouldn't think so," Goody said. "People tend to get offended when someone holds up the mirror of hypocrisy to their faces, and they are forced to acknowledge just how terrible they've let themselves become. That's what happens when people believe without questioning. Maybe you won't write it here. But maybe someday, you will."

"You speak as if you're leaving Home. I'm afraid the only way I'll leave is if I get sent the Hard Labor camp. I don't think I'll be writing any books there."

"One day we will leave, Suzannah," Goody said, suddenly pensive. "Perhaps not for a while, but one day." Goody shook her head, her thoughts returning to the present. "I think it's time for you to go back to the Handmaiden House." She kissed my forehead and stroked a strand of stray hair out of my face. "Good night, my dear."

"Good night, Goody," I said. Contentment washed over me. I felt loved; special. This woman took the time to talk to me, to listen to me. I walked back to the Handmaiden House, wondering what my life might have been like if my own mother treated me the way Goody Maars did. I wondered what Home would be like if husbands treated their wives and children the way Dr. Maars treated his.

I crept to my bed, undressed and slipped beneath the covers. That night I slept without dreams.

The next morning the kitchen matron shoved a note into my hands: the words 'sausage and bread' were scrawled across the card. It was the first time Silas had ever asked me to prepare something different from, what everyone else is having. I was thrilled to prepare his breakfast. I fried a single serving of sausage and sliced a generous portion of bread from the loaf, then carried it out to the table.

I arrived at the table to see an extra plate set.

"Who is the plate for?" I asked Goody Maars.

"Elder Morris is joining us this morning," she said. "You will be serving him today, as well as Silas."

So, the sausage and bread are for Elder Morris, not Silas, I thought, suddenly dejected. I would be happy to serve Silas anything he asked for. He had never raised his hand to me. I found no joy in serving Elder Morris. All I could think of was him slapping me before the pyre and Silas defending me.

The men arrived and stood at the table until Elder Morris arrived. Once he was seated, Dr. Maars and the other men sat.

"Suzannah, if you'd please," Morris said, gesturing towards the sausage and bread I had prepared.

There was an odd silence among the family. Dr. Maars stopped Goody at two spoons full of protein mush but didn't encourage her to eat.

"Momma, aren't you going to…"

"Shh, Telly," Goodwife Maars whispered.

Morris glared at the child.

"I'd prefer this to be toasted," Morris said to me,

gesturing towards the bread. "With butter."

"Yes, sir," I said. I took the bread from his plate and carried it back to the kitchens. I put the bread into the oven to toast it, slathered butter on it and returned.

Elder Morris was deep into conversation with Dr. Maars. "…if there's something wrong with the woman, there's something wrong with the child. You'll always see it in dogs, you see it with women."

"That's not always the case, Elder," Dr. Maars said.

I served Morris the toasted bread, trying my best to be unobtrusive. "This is… adequate, Suzannah. Next time, I'd like the bread a little softer on the inside."

"Yes, sir."

"Now, take the girls in the hard labor camps. Few of them have Elders for fathers," Morris continued.

"Are you saying that the daughters of anyone below the rank of Sub-Elder are not suitable for marriage?"

"If they were suitable, would they be sinning to the point of losing their purity? Their brains are too small to think properly. These are the women who are appropriately sent to the labor camps. It is best for our commune that such idiocy is bred out of the women in this population."

I felt faint, and more than a little angry. Dawn was not an idiot. Neither was Tessa. They were abused, broken, ready for death, but they were not stupid. Many of the girls in the hard labor camps bore the last name Commons. They were my cousins. Was I next in line?

Goody Maars grabbed my arm and supported me. She saw me almost collapse.

"I dare say that some of them aren't as sinful as we make them out to be," Dr. Maars said between mouthfuls of mush.

"Every girl has sinned, Dr. Maars," Morris said as if

the fact was so obvious only the dimwitted could not see it. "Their very existence is a disgrace."

"It sounds like you're arguing for men to lie with men," Dr. Maars replied, sounding bored.

"You know that's a perversion and a sin before the Master's eyes!" Morris cried. "It's equal to a woman not being a virgin before her marriage or killing someone!"

"You're talking in circles Morris," Dr. Maars said. "To insist women are so inferior they don't deserve to live, is to consign mankind to the grave. Only the female can give birth."

"You remember what happened ten winters ago, Ephraim."

Dr. Maars bristled. Silas stopped eating, his spoon halfway to his mouth.

"I do," Dr. Maars finally answered.

"It's a good thing that's outlawed now. Young men have an outlet for their needs, and girls have work to do to keep them too tired to fornicate. If they do, they get put in their place." Morris smiled as if he has scored the winning point. "By the by; I heard your son doesn't go with his troop to the Hard Labor camp. I hope there's nothing…wrong…with him," he added as if Silas wasn't seated next to him.

"Silas does not go to the Hard Labor camp because I've ordered him not to" Dr. Maars replied, his calm demeanor reasserting itself. "I insist that he abstain; it'll make for a better marriage."

"All this time with no outlet?" He burst out laughing and pounded Silas on the back. Silas's cheeks were turning red. "It might be good for a marriage but it's can't be good for you, son. If you hold it in too long, you'll explode!"

"I'll do my best not to explode, Elder," Silas

answered. "I find that I can channel that drive by focusing on my studies."

"Yes," Dr. Maars added. "I've been teaching Silas medicine, so he can replace me when the time comes."

"That is wise. Home will always need a trained physician," Morris nodded. "Has he witnessed a birth, yet?"

"I'm considering training Suzannah as the next midwife," Dr. Maars answered. "I believe she could make an excellent one."

Morris chuckled. "Really? You should set your sights higher, doctor!" My cheeks burned, whether with anger or embarrassment, I wasn't sure. Morris ate the last bite of the toasted bread, then announced, "We're done eating now. You women have permission to sit down now."

I took a seat, wedged been Morris and Silas. I waited as Goody Maars served herself - a sparse serving of mush - then she served Telly. When the bowl came to me, I put in one scoop, then went for another; I was so hungry.

"Stop," Morris ordered.

After my time serving the Maars and eating at their table, I was shocked by the command. I started to argue, to tell him I was hungry, but a warning glance from Goody made me bite my tongue.

I set the serving spoon back down.

"I decided I wanted some more," Morris said, taking the last few spoons full for himself.

I ate my portion in silence. My stomach rumbled, feeling half-empty. I had become accustomed to receiving equal portions. I forgot this was not the normal way of doing things in Home.

I hoped Morris doesn't return at the midday meal.

"The reports I hear of you going down to the Hard Labor camp in the early mornings with your wife make me uneasy," Morris said to Dr. Maars.

"They are still members of this commune," Dr. Maars said. "Our system would collapse if not for them."

"They are exiled for their sins. They're lucky to get a portion in the food they harvest."

"A minuscule portion," Dr. Maars shook his head. "It's hardly enough for them to survive. They're all suffering from malnutrition and disease. What happens if the all die? Who would do the hard labor then?"

Morris burst into laughter. "You speak as if those whores have value. If they all died tonight, by tomorrow we could find plenty of other girls to take their place. There is sin enough among the inhabitants of the Handmaiden House. Judgment is swift."

"Innocent girls? Punished for nothing?" Dr. Maars stared at the Elder, incredulous.

"Innocent? Not in the slightest!" Morris cried. "Women are forever in a state of sin. They *are* sin. Those who haven't been judged guilty simply haven't had their sins come to light, yet. I don't understand you, Doctor. You take your wife with you to that den of iniquity, surrounded by all those fallen girls. Aren't you worried they'll infect your wife with their sin?"

"I don't understand you, Elder," Dr. Maars countered. "You insist the militia boys visit the Hard Labor camp regularly. Aren't you worried all those sinful women will infect the men with they iniquity?"

Morris twisted his mouth into a grimace. "You speak of things that are too spiritually deep for you to understand," he answered at last.

"Enlighten me, Elder," Dr. Maars replied, without a hint of cynicism in his voice.

The two men locked eyes for a moment before Morris looked away.

"I think it might be best if you stayed away from those filthy whores," Morris said at last.

"For the sake of my conscience and for good of Home, I can't do that," Dr. Maars said.

"Out of the love of the Great Master, Ephraim," Morris swore. "They're only whores. It's not as if they were mankind."

Elder Morris joined us for the midday meal. And of course, he wanted something different than everyone else was eating. I worked hard to prepare his special meal, but if I expected any thanks, I would be disappointed. Morris treated my service as if it were his right, and I should be thankful for the opportunity to serve him.

"Suzannah," Silas said. "You've done a fine job preparing the meal."

"Don't flatter her," Morris reprimanded. "She's done an adequate job. Her food preparation skills are obviously lacking. But she has not complained and she serves from the right. At least she hasn't spilled anything on me, yet. That is commendable. Now, Suzannah, I'd like for you to cut a slice of meat off that lamb bone and feed me."

I was stunned. I had fed babies before, many times. But I had never had a grown man require this of me. I looked from Goody to Silas to Dr. Maars. Silas looked as furious as I felt, while Goody and Dr. Maars appeared merely exasperated, as if in the presence of a particularly petulant child.

I did as Morris commanded. I brought the fork to his

mouth and he took meat into his mouth. There was something malignant and hungry in his eyes that went beyond his appetite for food. My eyes met his for only a brief moment. I shivered.

"Cut a smaller piece next time, Suzannah," he chided.

"Yes, sir," I mumbled. I brought the next bite to his mouth, but he held up his hand for me to pause.

"Silas," Morris said, "I'm going to visit the Hard Labor camp tonight. You'll join me."

Silas's hand clenched into a fist around the handle of his fork, and Goody and Dr. Maars looked as if they'd both jump out of their skin. Goody gasped at the order. Silas remained calm. "I'm honored by your invitation, Elder, but I have medical studies I must attend to."

"Nonsense! You'll learn far more at the Hard Labor camp than you'll ever learn from your medical guides," Morris said, dismissively.

"My son said that he doesn't want to go," Dr. Maars said in monotone.

"Why Dr. Maars, I'm afraid you've mistaken my command for a request," Morris said darkly.

I now understood why Morris was sitting with us; he was here to establish Deacon's orders and expectations. He was here to crush the Maarses.

"Suzannah," Morris leered. "You may resume."

I lifted the fork to his mouth. He chewed slowly, savoring the flavor of the meat. The men ate the rest of the meal is silence. When the women were finally allowed to sit, Morris stood and laid his hand on my shoulder.

"My wife has just given birth for the third time," he said. "She needs some assistance with keeping the house. You will come by tonight after dinner and clean our quarters and gather our laundry."

"Yes, sir," I murmured. I didn't mind the extra work so much, but it saddened me that I wouldn't get to hear how *Jane Eyre* ended.

Morris stood. "Suzannah, come with me," he said.

I had just raised the fork to my mouth. Breakfast had been little and long ago. I was ravenous.

"May I eat first?"

"No," the Elder said.

Silas seethed in silence as I laid my fork beside my plate of uneaten food, and I followed Morris out. We walked past the Elders' wing, all the way down to Deacon's office. I had hoped to never see that room again. Morris knocked once, then opened the door.

Deacon sat behind his desk. He was obviously expecting this. I kept my eyes cast down, not looking at him.

"Hello, Suzannah," he said. "Sit down."

I took the hard chair across from the desk, careful not to make eye contact. I felt Morris's presence behind me. He slid his hands along my shoulders under the fabric of my tunic; his bare hands against my flesh. I shivered. He squeezed, to my revulsion.

Deacon steepled his fingers, tapping his fingertips together as if pondering a deep mystery. He stared at me for a long, uncomfortable moment in total silence.

"Suzannah," he said at last. "I need to know that you're sorry for disrespecting Elder Morris."

I thought about Elder Morris and anger flared up in my soul. My face flushed. I hoped Deacon would think it a blush of embarrassment and repentance. Goody had told me to play along, that eventually, they would take me out of Home, to the Ruins and beyond. *Are you sorry for the deaths of Dawn and Tessa, and countless others?* I bit my lip to keep from making a dreadful retort.

"Well?" Deacon asked.

"Yes, sir," I replied. "I'm very sorry for disrespecting the authority of the Elders. With your guidance, I'll learn to ignore my sinful nature and think only of my future husband's needs and my path in the Great Master. I hope to make a good wife someday."

"Very good." Deacon smiled. I thought he looked like a vulture. "You saw Silas Maars naked in his quarters, and were sentenced to make recompense by serving Silas as a wife would work for her future husband. As it should be. How do you feel about this?"

Morris squeezed my shoulders again. I cringed under his touch.

"The Maarses are an interesting family," I said. I glanced up. Deacon was tapping his fingers together again, expectantly. "Silas rarely asks for anything outside of what is normal. I have embraced this opportunity to restore my purity."

Deacon nodded. "Very good. You will be rewarded by the Great Master for your attempts at the time of redemption. But there is still much to do before your purity is fully restored here on earth. I have decided that Silas isn't requiring enough from you. Therefore, you are to serve both Elder Morris and Silas for the time being."

Morris's hands inched up to the sides of my neck and then slid back down to grip my upper arms.

"I will serve him gladly," I said, hoping my voice didn't betray the revulsion I felt.

"Good," Deacon said. "Look at me, Suzannah." I lifted my eyes to meet his. Deacon was smiling. I could feel the power of his words. "I believe that you will one day soon have your purity fully restored. At that time, you will make a good wife. I'm proud of you."

CHAPTER 12

Once again Elder Morris requested special food to be prepared. I scrambled to finish all my regular tasks and hurried to the kitchen to make sure I fulfilled his request. Once all things were ready, I stood obediently by the table. Morris entered alone and sat at the table awaiting the rest of the Maars men. He did not speak a word to me. He didn't even look at me. It was as if I were invisible or simply didn't exist.

At last the Maars family arrived, but an awkward silence reigned over the table. No one spoke. I could sense the hatred radiating off Silas. If Dr. Maars regarded Morris at all, it was complete indifference. Deacon offered a blessing on the food, and we were allowed to serve our men.

"Morris, would you like me to cut your food for you?" I asked, avoiding eye contact.

"Elder Morris," he replied. "Or simply 'Elder' will be acceptable. And yes, you may serve me now."

I cut the roasted lamb he had requested, skewed it on the fork and raised it to his mouth. He slipped his arm around me, pulling me closer to him as I fed him his meal. Silas sat in silence, picking at his plate. My stomach growled and Morris laughed.

"If you do an adequate job, I'll allow you more food tonight," he told me.

I cast my eyes down. "Thank you, Elder."

"This food is better than the midday meal. Did you have help?"

"Yes, Elder. From the best cook in the kitchen," I answered.

"I want you to study from her," he said, bits of food spraying out of his mouth as he spoke. I felt myself losing my appetite as I watch him eat.

"Silas, I want you to come with me to the Hard Labor camp tonight after worship, while Suzannah cleans my quarters."

"No," Silas answered.

"No? I'm sorry. Did I say something to make you think that was a request? I'm an Elder, and you…you are only a common militia soilder," Morris retorted.

"I don't want to go," Silas said.

Morris turned to stare at Silas as if he were a curious scientific specimen he had never seen before. "You *'don't want to go,'*" Morris repeated. "Why?"

The color drained from Silas's face and his strong, squared jaw trembled. "I don't know how," he said.

Morris exploded in raucous laughter, banging the table with this fist. "No wonder they call you queer, boy!" His voice suddenly took on a friendly, encouraging tone. "Come on, son, I'll take you to them. It'll be good for you. You'll be glad someone made you bed one of them, and then you won't be the butt of every joke in the commune anymore."

Dr. Maars' face looked like a thundercloud.

I felt sick.

Morris turned to Dr. Maars. "Tell him to go, Ephraim. You'll be saving him from your brother's fate."

Morris stood and left our table. He turned and called back to Silas, "Remember, after worship tonight."

Silas's face was ashen. "Papa," he said. "Please?"

Dr. Maars closed his eyes and rubbed the bridge of his nose. "I'll don't know if I can stop this," he whispered.

"Papa..."

"I'll do all that I can," Dr. Maars promised.

The bell rang, reminding us that worship would start soon. I rubbed my already dry hands on my lap napkin, feeling more than helpless.

"Suzannah," Goody said, standing. I picked up dishes and followed her to the kitchens.

"What are they going to do?" I whispered as I loaded the dirty plates onto the counter for washing. "Please, don't let that man make Silas do that!"

"Suzannah, I can't promise anything," she choked out. I realized she was fighting to hold back unshed tears. "Ephraim can only do so much. If Morris has his mind made up, there isn't much we can do to oppose him."

"Please..."

"Suzannah Commons, do not gossip in here," the Kitchen Matron snapped. "Come here, girl, and leave the Goodwife alone."

I trembled, but obeyed, casting a final pleading look toward Goody. I dashed to the sinks and scrubbed the pots and pans until the bell rang again for worship.

Dismissed from the kitchen, I made a beeline for the Maarses' pew. Silas was serving at the altar tonight. He stood by the front steps, holding candles in both hands, his head bowed. I wondered what was going through his mind.

Telly climbed into my lap, unaware of the turmoil Morris has created in her family, but she could sense something was wrong. "Suzannah, are you okay?" she whispered.

How did you tell a little girl that her brother was going to be forced to do something atrocious tonight while she was getting a nightly bath and being put to bed by loving parents?

"I'm fine," I whispered back and squeezed her.

Noah's sat perfectly still. I could hear his breathing, labored and strained.

Noah knew.

He's too young to know, I thought, but somehow he does. I'm too young to know too, but I do. Why? Why does life have to be this way?

I didn't deserve this. Noah didn't deserve to know this. Silas didn't need to be forced to do this! Tears gathered in my eyes as Deacon preached about man's honor and woman's duty. I thought I might throw up.

After worship, Morris gathered Silas and me under his watchful eye and herded us back to his quarters. I wanted to tell Silas not to do it, to say no, not to go. But I couldn't. I was too afraid. My insides quaked.

Silas, please, if you have to do it, at least please, don't hurt them!

Morris opened the door and ushered me inside. "My wife has a list of things for you to do," he said.

I felt like crying as I stepped inside the door. I thought Morris was a horrible person. I had yet to truly get to know his wife.

"Girl," the woman in the rocking chair shouted. She looked frazzled, angry, worn. She rocked back and forth, a colicky baby in her arms. "Get the broom and sweep this floor. It's filthy."

"Yes, ma'am," I said. I kept my eyes lowered. I fetched the broom and bent to my work. Two small children, playing with hand-sewn dolls, stared up at me. I tried to smile at them, but couldn't find the energy.

Morris's wife, Cassandra, barked orders at me the rest of the evening when she wasn't screaming at the children for being too loud or not sharing or for just being children. I'm not sure I had ever been as relieved as when she finally dismissed me. I collected my laundry sack and left for the Maars quarters to complete my work there. When I thought about what Silas had to do, I started weeping.

Tears were streaming down my face by the time I knocked on the door of the Maars quarters. Goody opened the door and drew me into a hug.

"I prayed I would never see this day," she confessed through her own tears.

Dr. Maars wasn't home tonight, and Noah and Telly were already in their rooms.

"I need to gather their laundry," I said at last.

Goody sniffed and nodded. I shuffled into the boys' bedroom and started shoving the pile of dirty laundry into my bag. Noah lay in the bottom bunk, staring into the darkness.

"Do you know when Silas will be home?" he asked.

"No," I replied.

"What's happening to him?"

"I don't know."

"You have to know…"

"I don't know, Noah!" I shouted, then immediately clapped my hands over my mouth. I crossed to the boy, his lip quivering and tears filling his eyes. "I'm sorry! Noah, I am so, so sorry," I apologized, trying my best not to cry.

I heard the door to the quarters open, footsteps followed, and the door creaked closed. I heard Goody softly weeping. I forgot about the laundry sack and rushed into the main room.

Dr. Maars and Silas were there.

I ran to Silas and embraced him. I knew it was wrong, that it could get me flogged, but at that moment I didn't care. "What happened?"

"I was called to the Hard Labor camp," Dr. Maars explained. "Pneumonia, bronchitis, influenza. It will spread throughout the camp, and we'll see more deaths, many more deaths before this contagion runs its course, I can guarantee you that."

Dr. Maars said, tossing his case down on the couch, then collapsed into his chair rubbing his temples with his fingers, as if trying to chase away a headache...or a nightmare. "I spent the evening gathering mucus samples from all of the girls. I confess I took my time and probably collected more samples than was absolutely necessary. Morris finally became bored and left. He'd never force my son in front of me."

Silas broke away from me. "It's only a matter of time," he muttered. "They'll never leave me alone until I'm just like them."

"Silas!" I cried. He looked at me, the pain in those blue eyes palpable. I couldn't put into words how I felt, what I wanted to say to him. His eyes searched mine. I reached out to him and touched his cheekbone with the tips of my fingers. It felt like the blood in my veins had suddenly caught fire and blazed through me.

"Suzannah?" I felt Dr. Maarses' hand on my shoulder. "I think you need to go back to the Handmaiden House now. Good night."

I didn't answer. I didn't take my eyes off Silas. I just picked up the laundry sack and left.

CHAPTER 13

Morris's wife couldn't stand the sight of me. That much was clear. Although I did my best to please her, she kept my chore list short and dismissed me quickly. This allowed me to spend more time Maars quarters.

Dr. Maars resumed his routine of reading aloud each night. Silas volunteered to work extra night patrols so he wouldn't be available to go with Morris to the Hard Labor camp. I missed seeing him, but was relieved at his reasons. So was Goody.

Tonight was different. Silas walked into the room, still in full militia uniform. He was restless, pacing across the room.

"They dismissed me for the night," he muttered. "Morris will find out. He's going to drag me out there. I can feel it."

Gloom washed over me; and fear. I didn't want Silas forced onto a girl. *I don't want Silas taking any girl, other than me. Where did that thought come from?* My cheeks burned at the thought.

"Suzannah?" Dr. Maars stood and beckoned to me. "Can you come here for a moment?" I nodded and he took me back to his bedroom.

"Hold out your arm," he said, and I complied.

He wrapped my wrist is some kind of medical bandage that was connected to a wire.

"What are you doing?" I asked, trying to not be curious, like that cat who pawed the spider.

"I'm turning off your tracking chip."

"You can do that?"

A grim smile creased the doctor's normally placid face.

"I'm transferring the information from your chip to another tracking chip. That chip will remain here in our quarters. We're going to the Ruins tonight."

"But I'm due back at the Handmaiden House."

Dr. Maars nodded as if he had already taken that information into account. He crossed to the intercom and pressed the call button.

"*Handmaiden House,*" the Matron's voice came through the cracked black speaker on the wall.

"This is Dr. Maars," he said. "Suzannah has become ill. She is running a fever and I'm afraid she may be contagious. I'm going to keep her under my wife's care in the infirmary this evening."

"*Are you sure you don't want to return her to us?*"

"I'm sure. I would not want the other girls, or you, to get this virus. It's not too harsh on young people, but it has a tendency to be particularly nasty to persons who are a bit older, such as yourself. But of course, if you wish for me to send her back to you…"

"*No! No, that's fine. You keep her as long as you think necessary. Thank you, Dr. Maars. Good night.*"

"Suzannah," Telly cried, bouncing on her tiptoes. She leaned close to me and whispered, "We're going to the Ruins!"

"I'm going to get my drawings," Noah said, as soon as his transfer was complete.

Silas entered and had his ID chip transferred.

"He's a really good artist, Suzannah," Silas said.

"We're going to the Ruins; we're going to the Ruins!" Telly repeated in a sing-song rhythm. Goody had to hold her still while Dr. Maars transferred her microchip's information. *"We're going! We're going, we're going!"* Telly sang.

Once everyone's tracking chip information was safely transferred, Dr. Maars picked up his bag, nodded to Goody, and led us to the storage room at the back of their quarters. I had never had a reason to enter this room before. I always assumed it was filled with medical supplies. When Dr. Maars opened the door, I was surprised to find a long, dimly lit corridor that dead-ended in a staircase that only went down.

We stepped single file down the stairs and into a wide basement. The air was stifling. Sweat popped out on my forehead and dripped down into my eyes. Dr. Maars strode across the basement, past the furnaces that were creating the oppressive heat in the room, to a door that, if you didn't know it was there, you wouldn't know it was there. He fished a key out of his bag, unlocked the door and ushered us into a small, dark room.

"Where are we?" I whispered. "I've ever been here before?"

"This entire complex used to be a prison for the mentally ill," Dr. Maars explained. "When an inmate died, they'd take the body to the furnaces and incinerate it. They used this elevator to avoid taking the body through the main complex where other prisoners might see it and get distressed."

"But, how do you know about this place?" I asked.

"I read about it in a book, from the library."

Silas shut the accordion bar door and the outer doors

came together of their own accord, as if driven by an unseen force. We stood in that tiny room in darkness, with only the number "1" glowing over the door, and the dim dots of light in tracking chips implanted on the back of our wrists, to illuminate the room. Only now they were glowing red, not green, like I was used to seeing my whole life.

There was a sensation of uneasiness beneath our feet and the floor rumbled slightly. The glowing number "1" flashed off, replaced by a glowing "P1." The "P1" flashed off, there was a ding, and "P2" flashed on.

The door opened into a dark corridor, which was blissfully cool after the heat of the furnace room. Goody Maars turned on a flashlight to light our way. I turned back to see what happened when we left the elevator. The doors closed on their own.

"This isn't part of Home," I breathed.

"No, it's not," Dr. Maars agreed.

We crossed an expanse that was marked by tall pillars at regular intervals that extended from floor to ceiling. At the far end of the enclosure, Dr. Maars reached into his bag and pulled out his key ring. He selected one, inserted it into the lock.

He nodded at Goody, who turned off the flashlight. Once we were in total darkness, he pushed opened the door to the outdoors.

A pleasant breeze wafted across my face, carrying a lovely scent of flowers and cooling my brow. The moon was full and provide all the light we needed.

We truly are outside of the compound! I could see the fence and the lights, the guard towers alight in the distance.

"Don't worry," Goodwife Maars said.

"They're not looking out here."

"If they aren't looking out here, to keep evil things from getting in, where are they looking?" I asked.

"They're looking inside the compound, to keep good people from getting out. Try to stay on the path, Suzannah. There are a lot of things you can trip over in the darkness and get hurt."

As if on cue, I tripped and fell.

I looked down and saw a small X, like the one that the Great Warrior had broken in half to be resurrected as the Roman Armies shot Him seventy times seven and stabbed Him just as many times; He broke it and died, then was resurrected.

I realized I had fallen on top of a grave. We were in a graveyard.

"Dead people are here," I whispered.

"Yes," Goody said as she helped me to my feet.

I looked around and saw all the grave markers; thousands, probably. The graves went on for what seemed like miles.

"This many people have died? One for every X?"

"Within Home, yes," she said.

"But, this isn't Home's graveyard," I said.

"Not anymore," Goody replied. "Not for a long time. Few people in Home even know this graveyard exists."

"This many people have died in Home?" I asked in horror.

Fewer than a thousand people lived in Home right now. I couldn't imagine what this meant at all. "Stars!"

There was a long silence. Dr. Maars turned around, and I saw the haunted expression on his face in the moonlight.

"How long has Home existed?" I asked.

"About a hundred and fifty years. The population has been in decline for many years," he said.

"Try not to think about it, dear," Goody Maars said. "It only hurts your head. And your heart."

I nodded and tried to be careful about where I stepped, and what I was stepping on. I wanted to be respectful of the dead.

Dr. Maars lead us through the back part of the courtyard along the trail to the woods. Telly was practically bouncing with excitement, but trying to keep quiet. Noah was more energetic, too.

We passed into a copse of tall pine trees, and the watchtowers of Home were blocked from our view. A deep sigh of relief washed over our party.

"On our way," Silas said as he handed me a flashlight from his satchel. I flipped it on and startled at the sudden circle of light that appeared in front of me. It took a moment for my eyes to adjust the fresh light.

"The woods are a little scary," I whispered.

"Not so scary without the threat of the reanimated or the Teeth," Goody whispered back.

"They're not real," I said, more than a bit perturbed at the deception being perpetrated on the common people of Home. "The reanimated dead and the Teeth; the never existed."

"No, I don't think so," Goody answered. "At least they have not existed in my lifetime. But all myths have some basis in reality."

"You mean, at one time they might have been real?" I asked.

"Cannibalism was recorded in the Old Testament in the Holy Book," Goody explained.

"Some books in the library tell of witch doctors in foreign lands who resurrected the dead through a practice called 'voodoo.' But we have plenty of other things to worry about tonight; things that are far more real, and no less dangerous, like wild animals."

"And landmines," Dr. Maars added. "Most in this area have been located and marked, although they can be hard to see at night."

I froze. The thought of stepping on a mine and having my legs blown off petrified me. "Is it safe to be out here, then?" I asked, suddenly wishing I was tucked away in my own little bed at the Handmaiden House.

"As safe as can we can make it," Dr. Maars said. "Just watch out for the little wire flags. They mark where an active landmine is buried."

Silas took my hand and encouraged me forward. Grateful for the human contact, I took another step, then another.

Dr. Maars wouldn't let Telly out here if it wasn't safe. What am I so afraid of? My fears started to recede when a low humming sound from ahead forced them back to the front of my brain.

"What's that?" I asked. "The noise?"

"It's nothing," Silas smiled in the darkness. "We'll show you."

The woods suddenly opened into a clearing where an old building, nearly obscured by weeds, stood. Dr. Maars reached into his bag and pulled out a small device with multiple buttons. He pushed one and lights appeared through the building's windows.

"What is this place?"

"This is the carriage house," Dr. Maars said.

"The carriage house?" I murmured, confusing clouding my thoughts. "Do they keep horses here?"

"In a manner of speaking," Dr. Maars chuckled. "The horses that power Home. We just need to drop some things off. Noah and Telly; stay outside, but don't go away from the door. We need to be able to hear you."

He unlocked the latch on the door and we walked inside. I was disappointed that there were no horses to be seen; only machines, humming.

"I thought the furnaces supplied the electricity for Home," I said.

"No," Dr. Maars said. "The furnaces produce heat. They don't generate electricity. Silas, the left corner."

Silas took off his backpack, unzipped it and pulled out something wrapped in plastic. Silas carried it to the corner, then called to me. "Suzannah, can you bring me a roll of tape from my backpack?"

I dug through the bag, found a roll of beige tape and carried it to him. I pulled out a length, then ripped it with my teeth and handed it to Silas. He taped it up the plastic-wrapped substance and stuck a wire into it.

"Suzannah, the tape please?" Goody Maars asked from Dr. Maars' corner.

I ran to their corner and tore a strip off for them. Silas called me away for more tape.

"What are we doing? What is this stuff?" I asked.

"Putty impregnated with nitroglycerin," he said. "Back in the old days, they called it, plastic explosive."

"Explosive? As in, we're going to blow up the carriage house?"

Silas grinned. "If we have to. It will create quite a distraction while we escape, don't you think? Another piece of tape please."

I tore it off and handed it to him.

"Suzannah?" Dr. Maars called.

I ran over to his corner and tore off another piece of tape for him. By the time we finished, there were plastic explosive packets in every corner of the room.

"Time to go," Dr. Maars said.

We found Noah and Telly drawing pictures in the

dirt by moonlight with a stick. Dr. Maars locked the Carriage House and turned off the lights with his device, but the building was still humming.

"The horses are still awake," I grinned, pleased with my joke. Silas smiled back at me, causing the butterflies in my stomach to take wing.

"Noah? Telly? It's time to go on to the car," Goody said. The two children dropped the stick.

"Yay!" Telly cried.

"I want my drawings," Noah whined.

"I don't think you'll be able to see well enough to draw, honey," Goody said, taking Telly's hand. "It's nighttime."

Noah pouted. "But I wanted to show Suzannah what I can do," he said.

"I would like to see your drawings, Noah," I tried to comfort him. "Are they like the drawing Telly made for me?"

"No," Noah said. "Second star to the right!"

"Not yet," Dr. Maars said.

"I don't understand. What does that mean?" I asked.

"We'll show you. When the time's right."

We marched back into the cover of the wooded path, with me and Silas bringing up the rear. He slipped his hand into mine and my cheeks burned. He lifted a finger to his lips, indicating I should be quiet, and we both smiled. I liked the feeling of his hand against mine. Nobody else saw it, or if they did, they didn't seem to care.

Noah pointed at something and turned around. "Second star to the right?" Noah questioned.

"And straight on 'til morning," the doctor finished.

I realized what they were looking at; two stars carved into the two tree trunks in front of us. Both contained initials carved into the bark; **EOM** and **MAC**.

"Two stars," I noted.

"That's how we remember it," Goody smiled, a little shyly, I thought. She gave Dr. Maars a quick kiss, then we turned and took the path that led to the right of the trees.

"They carved those stars when they were about our age," Silas told me.

Silas's parents were in love when they were our age? That means, what I'm feeling might be...normal?

Inside the commune, I was a Commons. Out here, under the stars, in the midst of all these trees, I felt like a Maars. I trusted them. And I knew I was right to trust them. I was not afraid here. There were no cannibals roaming the countryside; no reanimated corpses. I felt foolish for having ever believed such nonsense. Then again, I had never been told any different.

How many things have I been taught; how many things do I still believe that aren't true? The thought came unbidden, and I found myself growing angrier by the moment.

We came to a fork in the trail.

"*I shall be telling this with a sigh,*" Dr. Maars said.

"*Somewhere ages and ages hence,*" Silas added. "*Two roads diverged in a wood.*"

"*And I, I took the one less traveled by,*" Goody said.

"*And that has made all the difference,*" Silas and his father said together.

My anger turned to confusion. Both directions looked completely untraveled. How were we to determine which was less traveled?

"What road do we take?" I asked.

"Both lead to the same place," Silas grinned. Then he added, "But the one on the left is the shortest."

We started down the left path, and walked in silence.

"*The woods are lovely, dark and deep, but I have promises to keep and miles to go before I sleep. And miles to go before I sleep,*" Goody Maars intoned, jarring from my reverie. She was standing beside a pile of stones. I assumed they were a marker of sorts.

"We're leaving the path, now," she said to me. The others seemed to know the way. "Watch your step."

Goody reached out and took the hands of her younger children. She appeared happy to be doing so as if enjoying the freedom of expressing her love for her children without fear of disapproval. She received many frowns and disgusted glances for doing the same thing in Home.

Everything was so different out here. Goody's voice was stronger, her posture was straight and tall, even her demeanor was lighter. She was a different person.

Am I a different person out here? I certainly felt different, yet still the same. It was confusing.

We walked for what seemed a long way in the dark, disorienting woods with only the light of our flashlights, and I was about to ask Dr. Maars how much further when we stopped at another building. No hum came from this structure. It seemed completely abandoned; dead. I shivered.

"What is this?" I asked.

"Just a house," Doctor Maars said. "Nobody lives here now." He paused for a moment, pensive, then said in a low voice, "No one has lived here for a very, very long time."

I stepped forward to explore. I peered into a broken window. The place was indeed abandoned, forlorn. Chilly, blue lights flashed behind me and I whirled around to see Dr. Maars, Goody, and Silas pulling back a net sewn with multi-colored pieces of cloth that resembled leaves. We had walked right past it, and I didn't know it was there.

Beneath the net was a rusty, circular contraption, which was the source of the glowing blue lights. It was unlike anything I had ever seen. It had several cracked windows and one opening where the window was completely gone. The door handles were hard rubber like the pot handles in the kitchen.

"It's a hover car," Dr. Maars said.

"A hover car? That's not possible! Cars are made up legends." I shook my head. So many things I believed to be true were not; so many things I thought were made up stories were true. My world is upside down!

"The Americans left it to us to use."

"What are 'Americans'?" I asked. "I have so many questions!"

Dr. Maars just shook his head. He touched a lever on the hover car and a door sprang open.

"Come on, get in," was all he said.

Silas gestured for me to get into the back with him. I did as he indicated. The hover car was amazing, more incredible than I could have ever imagined. The inside glowed blue. The seats were smooth to the touch and soft to sit on, although there were few tears in the material where some kind of solid-foamy substance protruded out.

Telly piled into the backseat between me and Silas, and Noah climbed in on the other side.

"I've never... how is this possible?"

"There used to be hundreds, even thousands of them. Ordinary people use to operate them," Silas said. "They were made in a factory, like those pictures I showed you of women building airplanes."

"Only the smartest man in the world could have created this," I whispered.

"Actually, a woman designed this model," Dr. Maars said as he prepared to operate the craft.

"Women created this?" I whispered, shocked.

"Yes. Women and men, working together," Goody Maars said. She turned around in the front seat to smile at me. "It is amazing what we can accomplish when we treat each other as equals, don't you think?"

My jaw dropped. It was too much for my mind to conceive. "It would be different," I admitted. "We could do more. We could be... *more.*"

"Papa," Telly cried. "Let's go!"

"Patience, Tellulah," Dr. Maars admonished his youngest. "This is not a toy."

"I love riding in this," Silas said. "You'll love it, too."

"Why don't you sing your song, Telly?" Goody suggested. "It will help pass the time while we wait."

"*We're going to the rusty, rusty, rusty, rusty ruins!*" Telly sang. Noah joined in on their song. The children wriggled in their seats, laughing loudly as Dr. Maars started the hovercar. He donned special glasses that helped him see in the moonlight.

The seat underneath me vibrated and there was a violent rumble. It's not working, I thought for a moment, but the car lifted off the ground. I gasped as the car floated above the trees, although no one else seemed to find this unnatural.

Dr. Maars operated the controls moving the vehicle forward. My stomach was in my throat for a long moment but then settled as we gained speed. I stared, fascinated, out the window as the trees beneath us blurred by. *This is simply not possible!* The wind blew hard across my face through the broken window.

"Suzannah, please check and see if the commune is still visible," Dr. Maars called.

"Which way?" I asked. I was so disoriented at that moment I wasn't sure which way was up.

"Behind us," Silas said.

I turned to look, wondering if I would see the lights of Home. The wind whipped my hair around my face. I had never felt the wind like this in my life, either, even in the windstorms. It felt like I was flying. And then the reality hit me. We were flying! It was magic! Mankind could fly, I was one of them! It was exhilarating. It was terrifying, but I loved it! I had never felt so free.

I looked for any lights that might be Home. I saw them, tiny dots of light in the darkness; far, far away. I brushed my hair out of my face.

I said. "I can still see it."

"Thank you, dear," Goodwife Maars said.

"Judging the level of pollution, I'd say was two miles away," Dr. Maars replied.

We traveled in silence for a time; Telly's excitement had subsided a bit and she leaned her head against me. It felt lovely.

"Suzannah, please check again," Goodwife Maars said. I turned to look but could see no lights behind us. We were completely in darkness.

"I can't see Home anymore," I said.

Dr. Maars nodded, then flipped a switch. Light from the outside of the hovercar beamed down on the ground below us, and the interior glowed a soft blue. All I could do was marvel at the inside of this car.

Beneath us I saw what appeared to be a dark, double river, running side by side through the tree. Only it wasn't water. As I looked closer I realized it was a road, two roads, but it was old, the pavement pitted and broken with trees encroaching on it. The forest is reclaiming its lost property. In a few more years it will completely disappear. No one will even know it had ever existed. The thought made me sad somehow.

"How did people build such a long road?" I asked.

"It's called a highway," Dr. Maars said. "In the old days people paid taxes to the government and the government used that money to build things, like highways, for the common good. This highway allowed people to travel from city to city, from state to state."

"I don't understand," I said. "What do you mean, from state to state? People were allowed to travel beyond the limits of their commune?"

Dr. Maars sighed. "There was a time when people could travel where ever they wanted, whenever they wanted, without asking permission of anybody. Back then, this region was part of The United States, a union of fifty individual states. But there came a time when the people in the states where we live now didn't want to be a part of the United States anymore."

"Why," I asked, stunned. How could people turn their back on such marvelous advances? "If they could build something so wonderful, why would they want to stop being a part of it?"

"I don't know," Dr. Maars admitted. "There are few books in the library that were printed after 1995. I have found no mention of the United States after the year 2007. There was a war."

"Why?"

"I don't know," he admitted. "But it has happened before. A number of the states seceded from the union once before, and there was a war that forced those states to rejoin the union. But after another hundred years, give or take, they decided they didn't like the nation's leadership, so they left again. There was another war, much worse than the first. Much of the population was wiped out. The United States left us alone after that."

"We won the war?"

"No, Suzannah. There are no winners in wars," Dr. Maars said darkly. "Just a lot of dead soldiers. Just a lot of dead innocent bystanders. And a lot of widows and orphans, and pain and misery."

"The area was devastated by the war, the population reduced to pockets of humanity, mostly women and children," Goody explained. "Most of the region's men were killed during the war; a lot of women soldiers, too. That's how the commune system formed, with deacons and elders to guide us, to provide safety and security for those pockets of humanity that survived.

"In some places, it has served their people well, I suppose. In Home, it has proved to be just the opposite, leading to oppression and repression. Home is a perfect example of the old saying, *Power corrupts, and absolute power corrupts absolutely.*"

Silence held sway for a long time after that as I pondered Goody's words.

"The Ruins are really pretty," Telly said suddenly. "I can't wait to show you, Suzannah."

"There are statues inside a circle," Noah said. "They're really pretty, too."

"They're not really all that pretty," Silas snarked. "They're just naked. that's why you like them."

Everyone in the car laughed except me.

"Naked? But that's wrong!" I cried, horrified.

"These statues are art," Goody Maars said.

"Art makes it okay?"

I pictured obscene statues of people, uncovered and exposed.

"Art challenges the mind. It shows the soul," Dr. Maars said.

"It's just the body, unadorned," Goody Maars said. "There's nothing wrong with it. It's not always carnal. It's just the way the human form is. The human body is quite beautiful and mysterious. The Great Master created our bodies as works of art; specially made, carefully molded."

"Why," I asked, confused.

Goody paused a moment. I could see her cast a loving glance toward her husband. "I believe He does it to remind us of how important we truly are to Him."

We were important to the Great Master? I had never heard such a thing before. It was outrageous.

"We're all important to God," Silas added. "That's what He's called in the holy book. *God. Yahweh. Father.*"

"But, we call him the Great Master," I commented, my confusion mounting by the moment.

"Yes. And He is the Great Master," Silas said. "But He is so much more than that."

"People can change their perception of a thing by focusing on only one attribute," Dr. Maars sighed. "By only focusing on God's attribute as the Great Master, the deacons and elders of Home have turned Him into little more than a slave-owner, and they've turned the people of Home into unwilling slaves. But the Holy Book says He is... so much bigger than our human brains can comprehend. It describes Him as ...a father; not a harsh, judgmental father, but as a kind and loving one. One who provides for His children, to cares for them, teaches them and defends them...one who would willingly lay down His life for them."

Like you, I thought, but didn't dare say.

Dr. Maars' tone changed. "Our Deacon and Elders

have made a god in their own image, to suit their own needs," he spat. "I find it disgusting."

My jaw dropped.

"Now, dear, she hasn't read the Bible yet," Goody said.

"I've read the Holy Book," Silas chimed in. "It's an amazing book. So much history and so many challenges. I don't understand why Deacon doesn't simply speak the words written in it. Why not give the people the freedom to think for themselves?"

"Because knowledge is power," Goody answered. "And what Deacon craves above all else is power."

The car was silent for a moment.

"You've got this," I said, indicating the hovercar. "You could leave anytime you want. Why haven't you already left?"

"It's not that simple," Dr. Maars said. "There is more to consider than just our family's well-being. But someday. The time might come when we have to."

I felt a knot in my stomach and my heartbeat quickened. "Don't!" I cried.

"Don't what?"

"I don't want you ever leaving. Please don't leave!"

"You actually think we'd leave without you?" Goody Maars asked, turning around in her seat to look at me. "We'd never do that."

"You wouldn't?"

"That's what families do: we'd never separate if we didn't have to."

"It's true," Silas said.

"I'd never want you to be alone without me," Telly said, wiggling into my lap.

"Me neither," Noah said.

My heart climbed back into my throat, and this time it had nothing to do with the speed the hovercar was traveling. I had never associated family with these feelings. I wiped away a stray tear, and we traveled on in silence.

Tall buildings appeared against the night sky as we neared the Ruins, like tombstones against the horizon. Like the graveyard, I thought. My jaw dropped at the sheer size of these massive structures. Men built these? Amazing!

"That's the Batman Building," Noah pointed to a tall building with two spires extending even higher.

"What's a Batman?" I asked.

He shrugged. "I dunno. It's what the Americans called it."

"Do they come here a lot? The Americans?"

"Occasionally," Dr. Maars answered. "The United States sends researchers here to check pollution levels."

Dr. Maars slowed the hovercar and allowed it to drift toward the ground while navigating along the deserted highway into the ruined city.

"This place used to be full of cars, like that one," Silas mused, pointing to a box-like contraption that sat rusting in the middle of the road. "They traveled on the ground. Can you imagine it?

Dr. Maars turned off the main highway onto a side road, and we passed through a corridor of crumbling buildings with broken out windows. I saw a sign with an odd, unknown word written on it.

"Demon-brun," I tried to sound it out. "Is that how it is pronounced?"

Goody nodded. "Close enough," she said. "At one time all these streets had names. Some were named after influential people, others for common objects."

Dr. Maars piloted the hovercar through several twists and turns, each new vista revealed more wonders. I gazed at the crumbling buildings in awe. So many people must have lived here, I thought. I couldn't even imagine how life must have been back then.

It must have been very crowded. How could so many people live so close together?

Yet there was a strange beauty about these old, dead buildings. Many of them had writing scrawled on their walls and pictures.

Dr. Maars allowed the hovercar to drift down to the street. Once it had completely settled, he turned a switch, and all the lights went out. It was as if they hovercar had been a living thing, and was now dead. I felt a twinge of sadness.

"Come on," Silas said. "Let's get out."

"Is it safe? What about the hovercar?" I asked, "Are you sure there's nobody here?"

"Other than a few wild animals, feral cats and that sort of thing, I think we're probably fine," Goody said. "Many years ago there were some scavengers who passed through, but we haven't seen any other humans, other than the Americans, in a very long time."

"There they are!" Noah shouted, pointing. He ran ahead of us in the dark without a thought for safety.

"Noah, wait," Goody shouted. She jogged after him with her flashlight, trying to avoid potholes as she chased after her son. I ran after them too. I wanted to see what Noah was going towards.

"Found it!" Noah shouted, waving his arms over his head and jumping up and down. We joined him on a round street. I was confused. I had never seen a road that went in a circle. *What could possibly be the purpose of that?* I wondered.

As we drew closer the beam of my flashlight revealed a platform in the center of the pavement, and statues were on the platform. Like the buildings, they were crumbling. I lifted my flashlight to take in the full sculpture, then quickly whipped the light away. Silas had been right; the statues were people, men and women. And they were naked, indeed!

Noah got into the rusty remains of a car, opened the dashboard and pulled something out.

"What do you have there?" I asked, my curiosity overcoming my desire to avert my eyes.

"My drawings!" he cried. He ran to me and shoved several papers into my hands. "I did these myself!"

I lifted my flashlight and looked. I gasped again. Noah had drawn pictures of the naked statues.

"He's very proud of them," Goody said, laughed. "He's taught himself."

"But they're…naked. I can't look at this!"

"Alright. Then don't," Goody soothed, taking them from me gently. She handed them back to Noah.

"Mother, can I stay here and draw?" Noah asked.

"For a while. We're going to go check the Alley for the medicine."

"Why don't the Americans just leave the medicine here?" Noah asked. "It would be a lot easier."

"Too many questions," Goody said, kissing his forehead. "Come on, Suzannah. We'll leave Noah to draw. Sweetheart, if anything goes wrong, go back to the car and use this." She handed him something that was long and skinny and covered in paper.

"I will," Noah said. "Thank you, Mama."

Goody and I walked back to the hovercar where Dr. Maars and Silas were waiting. Telly played with a flashlight, dancing around to music no one else could hear.

"What did you think?" Silas asked.

I shook my head. "I don't think I'll ever understand it."

Dr. Maars interrupted. "Come on, we need to go to the Alley."

Goody sighed, looking back toward Noah and the sculpture. "I hate leaving him there by himself," she said. "So much could happen."

"Nothing ever has," Dr. Maars said. "We only have a few hours before the sun rises. Let's go."

As we walked together down the street, I peered into the abandoned building, trying to imagine people living and working in this once grand city. Everything was in a state of decay, yet there was such peace here, not at all like walking down one of the compound of Home.

The concrete was cracked and crumbling under our feet. I was so busy gawking at everything that I tripped a few times. Silas pointed to two structures in the distance – bridges, at least, what was left of them.

They glowed in the moonlight, like light beams. Someone had built that to span a river! I thought in wonder.

Silas pulled me down another street, 'Broadway,' he called it. I stared at a giant structure, the one I assumed was the Batman Building. From up close it looked about to collapse upon itself. It was covered in green, climbing ivy. Three feral cats saw us, hissed, then ran away. We followed Dr. Maars down yet another street.

"No wonder they named the streets," I said. "There are so many of them!" I grinned and tried to read the street signs in the moonlight. Some were numbers, others had names.

"Charlotte!" I cried out, pointing at a sign and clapping my hands.

"Yes," Dr. Maars nodded.

"Like Charlotte Brontë," I actually laughed aloud.

In Home, I always had to be so careful. Laughing loudly was considered unseemly. You couldn't look older people, particularly men, in the face. And you couldn't feel the way I felt about Silas. He made my stomach feel all fluttery. But here…here I could laugh, or shout, or dance, or look into Silas's eyes and nobody told me I was being sinful or threatened to switch me or send me to the Hard Labor camp.

Further down the street and saw an iron arch rusting over a street entrance.

PR   R'S ALL Y

"This is the alley, right?"

"This is it," Dr. Maars said.

"But, why are we here?"

"The Americans come here and leave us the medicines we ask for." Dr. Maars answered.

"What do you give them in return?" I asked

Dr. and Goody paused, looking at each other. "Information," Goody finally answered.

"Where're the stars?" Telly asked.

"We look for the stars," Goody explained.

"It's the sign they leave so we know where to find it," Dr. Maars explained.

"There," Telly cried, pointing. "In the window. Right there in the window!"

I saw something flapping in the broken window; some kind of dark material with white stars shining in the moonlight. We ran toward it. Silas picked it up to show me and turned it over. On the reverse side were red and white stripes. "This side tells the Americans that we've been here."

Silas helped Telly climb through the window. He

climbed in after her, then reached back for me. He took my hand and pulled as I climbed inside. I didn't want to let go, even though there was no longer a need for Silas to hold my hand.

The roof had collapsed in places and moonlight streamed through the holes. There were the decaying remnants of tables and chairs scattered across the room, and a long, long table top with the shattered remains of a mirror behind it.

"What kind of place was this?" I asked.

"It was a common room of sorts, I think," Silas said.

"Found it," Telly said proudly, lifting a box over her head.

"Good job, Telly," Silas called.

"Children," Goody Maars shouted from outside. "Be careful!"

"It's alright, Mother," Silas called. "We found it!"

"Come back out immediately, this building isn't safe! It could collapse at any moment!"

"The roof's already out," Silas said. He lowered Telly, still holding the box, out of the window, then helped me out before jumping down to the street himself.

"Telly found it this time," he told his mother.

I suddenly felt sad. Our mission was accomplished.

"Do we have to go back now?" I asked.

"Not right now," Dr. Maars said, and impish grin creasing his weathered face. He struck his flashlight beam onto Telly and shouted. "Flashlight tag! Telly's it!"

"Run!" Silas shouted.

I grabbed his hand and we raced down the street, together, laughing as we tried to avoid Telly's flashlight beam.

The game lasted for the better part of an hour. I was *It* several times. It was so much fun. I hadn't felt hat way since I was a little girl, long before I entered the Handmaiden House. I didn't want to leave.

I hid inside a building that was nothing but walls. Its ceiling was the moon and the stars. I laid back and let myself look up at it. I had never really looked at the moon before. We weren't allowed to. They said the Great Master lived up there and watched us. We were told it was sinful to try to watch back. But tonight, I saw the white crescent moon, and it was beautiful. There were tiny dots of light in the dark part of the crescent, and I wondered what they could be. More stars? And I thought things I had never thought before. Why wouldn't He want us to look up to Him, to adore Him?

I sat up and spotted something else. More stars hanging over a large, long desk. Is this more medicine? Did they leave the second package? I pulled the fabric out and beneath it was a light-colored box. It was more medicine. I was sure of it. Feeling proud to have discovered this second package, I decided to open it.

My eyes flew open wide. Instead of medicine, there were more of those beautiful heart-shaped cookies. I picked one up. It felt soft and fresh. I broke it apart and popped a piece into my mouth. I literally melted in my mouth, the sweet taste making me feel like I was floating. I moaned softly.

"Suzannah? Where are you?"

"Here," I answered.

Silas appeared in the doorway. "Find something?"

"Yes," I said, holding out the box for him to see.

"And you're planning on keeping them all for yourself?" Silas asked. I saw him grin in the moonlight.

"Maybe," I grinned back. "I just ate one."

"I won't tell. But you have to give me one."

"Here," I reached toward him, but he didn't take it.

"Put it in my mouth for me," he said. "My hands are dirty."

"And mine aren't?"

He opened his mouth and I realized he was serious. This was not like when Morris commanded me to feed him. This was something…different. This was…exciting. I broke off a piece of the pastry, and held it out to him, placing it on his tongue. His lips closed around my fingers. I jumped back and pulled my hand away. It felt like lightning had shot through my fingers, up my arm and straight down into my abdomen, setting my nerves on fire. I tingled from head to toe.

"Silas!" I giggled. "You can't do that."

But why can't he do that? I liked it. I liked the feeling of his lips on my skin. Was this what a kiss felt like? Kissing was forbidden except for married people. I imagined Silas kissing me and a fire exploded in the base of my stomach, an unfamiliar and exciting feeling that made my heart race. I realized I wanted him to kiss me; to kiss me full on the mouth.

Could I sacrifice my purity to Silas out here? Deacon would never find out. Was it possible? No! I could never do it.

Silas snatched the rest of the cookie from my hand and popped it into his mouth.

"We'll just tell them this is all we found," he said, wiping his face with his sleeve. "Come on." He took my hand again and led me out into the alley.

I heard something, like a bird's tweet, but not a bird; something soft and familiar, yet unlike anything I had ever heard before.

All I knew was I wanted to hear more.

"What is that?" I cried.

"Music," Silas answered.

"No. Music is when we sing hymns," I said.

"Music is more than singing," Silas said. "You've never heard instruments play before, have you?"

"What are instruments?" I asked.

"Instruments are things that people use to make music."

"But who is making the music? It's not us."

"It's called a recording," Silas explained. He smiled at the blank look that crossed my eyes. "I can't really explain it," he said. "You'll see."

He smiled as we walked out into the street, hand in hand. Telly was dancing in the moonlight, spinning twirling and giggling. To one side the doctor and his wife were standing close together, very close together. Her cheek was pressed against his chest and her hand was on his shoulder. He had his left arm around her waist and he held her hand in his right hand. They were swaying in time to the music.

I heard a voice, singing along with the music, but it wasn't a hymn. It was soft, and winsome, and fragile and it made me sad and happy at the same time.

"*Hear the lonesome whippoorwill,*" the voice crooned into the night.

The doctor cupped Goody's face with one hand turned her into a doorway.

"*He sounds too blue to fly...*"

He kissed her! And not like the way I ever saw anybody kiss in Home. It was something long, and drawn out, something that felt very, very private.

"*The midnight train is whining low,*"

A deep longing welled up inside me. I wanted Silas to do that to me.

"*I'm so lonesome I could cry.*"

I leaned back into Silas, and felt the warmth of his

body next to mine. I wanted to have a private moment like that with him. I wanted to explore these new feelings. I wanted to understand these new desires and curiosities. I wondered if he did, too. I wondered if husbands and wives got to explore each other in the privacy of their own quarters like I wanted to do with Silas.

I had seen him naked. The memory of what he had looked like made that intense sensation in my stomach burn harder. I wanted to feel this for another human being, to care for each other, to be consumed by desire for each other. Is this what love was? Was this fluttering feeling in my stomach when I was near Silas, the burn, the ache…love?

Perhaps I really wasn't so strange after all. This feeling didn't just happen to me. Other people had it; Dr. Maars and Goody Maars felt it. Maybe this is what made them so different from everyone else in Home... love.

No. I wasn't supposed to feel this way. It was forbidden. It was wrong!

"Silas," I heard myself gasp.

I didn't care if it was wrong; I wanted it! I wanted Silas. I could only hope Silas wanted me, too.

Silas had heard me breathe his name. He turned to look at me, and then we looked back at his parents.

"Suzannah?" Silas whispered. "Does it scare you?" he whispered.

I nodded. Then shook my head. I couldn't explain what I was feeling, what I was thinking. I was afraid, and exhilarated, and brave and terrified. I dared to reach up and touch his cheek.

I thought of his lips on mine. The thought made my cheeks burn and my head swim.

It was beautiful.

"The way I feel when I'm with you… it scares me too," Silas confessed.

"I'm afraid I'll never have that. With you. I want that," I whispered.

"You will," Silas whispered. He cupped my face in his hands. He hesitated for a second and then leaned in, his eyes closed. His lips brushed against mine, softly, tenderly. And I melted inside.

It lasted only a moment, but my heart was racing, pounding inside my chest. My stomach fluttered. My brain reeled. I reached my hand behind his head and drew his lips back down to mine again, this time longer and harder. I had never known a moment more beautiful.

We stepped apart. We stood there for…I don't know for how long, just looking into each other's eyes.

I didn't know that love existed before tonight.

It didn't exist in my tiny world of Home. Why did we have to go back? *Why can't we just stay here in the Ruins, and make a life for ourselves out here, away from Deacon and the Elders and the Hard Labor camp and the Handmaiden House?*

As soon as it started, the moment was over. Goody called to us, and we all trekked back to the hovercar. Telly was asleep on her feet. Dr. Maars gathered her into his arms and carried her the last few blocks. Silas and I walked together, hand in hand, through the deserted streets. Noah was inside the hovercar, sleeping when we arrived.

We rode back in the blackness that was common just before dawn, temporarily stopping in a field of wild poppies to grab a few blooms for a medicine they Maarses made to numb pain. Silas still held my hand in the back seat. I melted into him, soaking in the moment, trying to not think about having to hide my feelings for him. Visions of Silas kissing me rolled through my mind, bringing a smile to my face and that pleasant, giddy feeling in my stomach. I couldn't re-imagine that moment enough. It had been perfect.

How many perfect moments does a girl get? I wondered. Nothing could top that one, I was certain.

"Can we go back soon?" I whispered to Silas.

"Next month," Silas replied.

"You go every month?"

"Yeah. Just about."

"I want to go."

"I don't think we can sneak you out every month," Silas said.

"Maybe. Maybe I could make it happen," Dr. Maars said. I hadn't realized he was listening to us talking. Goody was in the crook of his arm, holding Telly, who was fast asleep, and her head stirred slightly.

I couldn't imagine being left behind when they went back to the Ruins. There was so much to explore there; the music, the buildings, the mystery. Most of all, I'd miss the magic of being close to Silas without everyone watching and judging me, worrying what other people thought. Worrying that someone would tell the Elders and Deacon.

By the time we stopped the hovercar the exhilaration of the adventure had worn off, and I discovered I was weary. I had been awake all night long. We walked through the graveyard, through the underground tunnel, and back into the Maars quarters.

The breakfast bell would ring soon. The Handmaiden House, the militia, and the hard labor camp would be waking.

And I would go back to my life here in Home.

I would stand it. I had to. I had seen the outside world and it was far better, far more beautiful than anything I could have imagined. And I knew for certain that I was in love with Silas Maars.

CHAPTER 14

The sizzle of my flesh awoke me from my daydream. I shrieked and dropped the hot iron. Luckily, it clambered to the floor and didn't hit me or anyone else.

"Stars above! Suzannah Commons!" the Laundry Matron shouted.

"I'm sorry," I apologized, shaking my hand. "I burned myself."

"Let's see, girl," she tsked, taking my hand. She examined the rising blister, then suddenly slapped it. "That's nothing. Barely a burn at all. Finish your work!"

I slipped some cloth around the handle, picked up the iron and resumed my chore. *Focus, Suzannah. Focus! You have to stop thinking about the Ruins and concentrate on your laundry quota.*

I rushed to get to the kitchen, where the Kitchen Matron handed me Morris's order; soup and toasted bread. I prepared it the way he preferred and brought it out to the Maars table just as Goodwife Maars and Telly entered the common room.

I looked upon Goody Maars as my own mother now; Telly as a little sister. I only wished Elder Morris would sit with his own wife, instead of at our table. I liked our little family.

After dinner and worship, I went to Morris's quarters and cleaned his wife's cot and the living area. Goody Morris, Cassandra, was busy nursing the new baby while the other two children ran through the quarters, playing with wooden figurines. The woman glared at me through slitted eyes. I didn't know why. I had never done anything to offend her that I knew of. I did my work without a word, carried her dinner dishes back to the kitchens, then went back to the Maarses' quarters, where Dr. Maars was already reading to his family.

I checked to see if Silas and Noah's room needed cleaning, but as usual, it was spotless. I went to the living room to sit down and Telly handed me a handkerchief with several of the heart-shaped cookies in it. "We saved these for you," she said.

"Thank you, Telly," I said, taking a bite. I had to remind myself not to eat them all and to save some for later.

Dr. Maars read for a few minutes more, then took his glasses off and sighed. "It's too much," he said, rubbing the bridge of his nose.

"What's wrong, dear?" Goody Maars asked.

"A headache. My eyes are strained. Silas? Can you read instead?"

Silas accepted the book and took up where his father left off. I wish someday that I can read aloud as well as Silas does. I could read, but I had to work at it. When Dr. Maars or Silas read, the words flowed off the page. Goody Maars left for a moment, then returned with some cool water from the distillery for Dr. Maars.

"I'm tired," Silas yawned.

"It's bedtime for Noah and Telly," Goody Maars said.

"I have a question."

"Yes, Suzannah?"

"Did the Americans leave you the hovercar?"

"They did."

"How did you meet them?"

Dr. Maars closed his eyes. "That is a bit of a long story," he said. "It was the year before we were married. Deacon visited the previous doctor, Marissa's father. He had been losing weight, getting headaches and having digestive problems. Upon examination, we discovered a mass the size of your fist in his stomach."

"It was cancer," Goody Maars said. "Papa could tell."

"Of course, he didn't want to hear it," Dr. Maars continued. "It was a death sentence. No one ever got cancer and lived for more than a year or so. We simply don't have the tools to effectively treat it."

"So, Deacon had cancer?"

"Has cancer, dear," Goody Maars said.

"He still has it? After all these years? How? I mean, how is he still alive?"

"That's our doing," Dr. Maars confessed. "We used to go in search of poppy fields to harvest the seeds. We used those seeds to create morphine to dull the pain, but he was getting worse. We like to have theme in stock, though.

"One day, while we were out in the field, a helicopter flew over head. It nearly scared us both to death. We had heard of such machines, but I had never seen one. Apparently, it saw us, and it landed, and Americans stepped out.

"We knew we couldn't out run them, and we had nothing to fight them with, so we surrendered. We expected them to torture us. Instead, they told us they were a research team, measuring the effects of pollution in the region.

"They told us many things about the outside world,

and we told them we were trying to make painkilling drugs for our leader.

"They took us back to the helicopter, retrieved a medical bag, and gave it to us. It contained life-saving drugs we had never even heard of. They said, in their country, they had drugs that could reduce and even cure cancer. They agreed to give us the medicine if Deacon would agree to take it. We parted, with an agreement to meet back at the same place in four weeks.

"We returned to the commune, gave Deacon the painkillers, and told him about the Americans' offer. He didn't like it, but their medicines brought him significant relief. He agreed to let us meet the Americans each month, as long as they brought medicine for him. Every four weeks since then we have trekked to the Ruins. And every four weeks we come back with medicine.

"That's what the Find the Stars game is; discovering where they hid the treatment. They left that old hovercar for us to use, but Deacon doesn't know this. We tell him that the Americans meet us in the woods every few weeks to deliver his treatment."

"So that's why he allowed the two of you to marry," I surmised. "He owed you. But Goody, what happened to your father?"

Goody and Doctor Maars exchanged a glance. "That's a story for another time. I think it's time for you to go home. Ephraim, would you walk her back to the Handmaiden House? It might be good for your headache to get some fresh air."

"Suzannah, let me help you with the laundry," he said, standing up.

As we left their quarters, he lifted the laundry sack over his shoulder.

"I'm sorry," I said. "I didn't mean to ask a stupid question."

"It's alright," he said. "It's just difficult for her to speak of. She was very close to her father, and we lost him the year after Silas was born."

I nodded and bit my lip. I know I shouldn't be so curious, but I couldn't help myself. I asked anyway.

"Can you tell me what happened?"

Dr. Maars blew out a deep breath.

"He was a good man," he said. "He encouraged me to read whatever I wanted from the library. He is the one who taught me medicine; he taught me and Marissa together – she was far more adept at it than I.

"He was shot."

My eyebrows raised and I stared at the doctor.

"Shot? By who?"

"The militia," he said. "He told us it was an accident, but I never believed him. The story was that he was treating one of the hard labor girls for a severe infection with a group of militia boys came in, carrying their guns. He told them to leave, but they insisted on staying. They set their rifles down, but one tipped over an accidentally discharged, the bullet striking Marissa's father in the gut.

"That's the story.

"Anyway, I got the call late that night. They brought him to the infirmary. We put him under anesthesia and staunched the bleeding as best we could, but I could tell he was bleeding internally. The bullet was lodged close to his spine. I couldn't get it out. He was going to die. All we could do was make him as comfortable as possible.

"He drifted in and out of consciousness for the next three days, then passed away. Marissa didn't sleep that entire time. The ordeal put a tremendous strain on her.

"She was pregnant at the time, and the day he died,

she went into early labor and gave birth to a baby girl. It almost killed her."

"You had another daughter?" I repeated, stunned.

"Yes." A bittersweet smile crossed the doctor's face. "Her name was Lana, and she was so…beautiful…but so very small. We tried so hard to help her survive, but she was quite early, and she just didn't have the strength to nurse.

"Some of the other mothers in Home came to help. Your mother was one of them. You had just been born. But, we lost her. She would have been the same age as you."

What could I say to such a story? I felt at a solemn loss for words. We walked on in silence for a few more moments. At last, I asked, "Is Lana buried behind Home?"

"Yes," Dr. Maars answered. "She is. I dug the grave myself." He sighed dejectedly. "We are not the only parents in Home who have lost a baby. Infant mortality in this commune is high, terribly high, perhaps one in ten pregnancies ends in miscarriage or the baby dies within the first few months of life."

I nodded as he walked me up to the door of the Handmaiden House.

"This is something that still makes Marissa sad," he continued. "Please don't bring this up with her again."

"I won't," I promised.

"Good. Sleep well and good night."

✛✛✛

I wiped my hands on the dish towel tied over my skirt as an apron as Morris conversed with Dr. Maars. I hated listening to that man talk. I resented Morris. I was repulsed by him. Yet I had to listen as he prated on and on about how stupid and inferior females were. The more he talked the angrier I became. But I was trapped. There was nothing I could do about it.

"Women have a genetic propensity to hysteria," Morris argued. "They need to be put back to work as soon as possible after giving birth. Otherwise, they are likely to do demented things to their babies when left alone with them."

"Pregnancy makes the body's hormone levels unpredictable," Dr. Maars countered. "It's the chemical imbalance that triggers such behavior in some women. Men would react the same way under the same circumstances. It's when they're left alone and told to deal with it-"

"All the more reason to put them back to work as soon as they're able to stand," Morris said. "It's uncomfortable, but should they really be spending so much time alone with their new babies when they're so inferior that they can't control their own emotions?"

Goody twisted her apron between her hand, wringing it, staring at the tiles on the floor. I reached over to touch her wrist, and she glanced over at me. I could see unshed tears in her eyes.

Dr. Maars sighed. "Such isolation with a newborn to care for can drive any one insane, male or female."

"It's a sign of weakness. A boy in isolation will never go insane. If he does, it means he's weak. Too weak to be a father or a husband. If I were that weak, I'd rather be stoned to death, Ephraim."

Dr. Maars' face clouded over. "I'm finished with my food. The women may join us now."

"Suzannah," Morris said.

I jumped. "Yes, sir?" I kept my eyes to the floor.

"Elder Chatson will see you, now. Go."

I hadn't eaten, but there was no use complaining.

That would only make things worse. I curtsied, left the dining hall and made my way down to the Elders' wing.

I stood outside Elder Chatson's office and realized I still had the dishtowel around my waist. I considered whether I should leave it in the hall until my meeting was over or just wear it in. I decided to wear it in. I knocked on the door.

"Yes?"

"It's Suzannah Commons." I said. "Elder Morris sent me."

"Come in."

I twisted the door handle, lowered my eyes to the floor, and entered.

"Suzannah." The Elder considered me. I could smell the food he had been served in his office; baked chicken and warm, fresh bread with cooked peas. I stood, my hands clasped in front of me, my stomach growling. He listened to it but said nothing for a long time. "You're doing quite well with your punishment at the Maars family's quarters. How have you liked it?"

This is a trick question, I thought. *He's trying to catch me in some kind of sin. He wants me to admit to it, and then he'll take me to Deacon to confess and get another punishment.* "It's been humbling," I answered. "I believe is is helping me get ready for my future as a wife."

I raised my eyes enough to see his desk top. He was tapping a pen against it. My heart thundered inside my chest. I was terrified. What does he know? Does he know about the book? The cookies? That I wasn't cleaning, but listening to Dr. Maars read books to us?

He stopped tapping his pen. "Do you think you're ready to be a wife, Suzannah?"

I pursed my lips. Saying 'yes' would seem prideful, but saying 'no' might sound disrespectful. "I'm only a woman, and such questions are too high for me, Elder. If you think I'm ready, Elder, then I am ready."

The pen started tapping again. My heart kept time to that horrible *tap, tap, tap.*

"I don't think you should work any longer for the Maars family."

I gasped, just barely remembering not to look at him directly.

"You like working for the Maars?"

"The Maarses are nice people," I admitted. "I think Dr. Maars is a good man."

"Would you like a husband like him someday?"

I bit my lips together. "He leads his wife and children very well. They respect him and mind what he says," I said, measuring my words carefully. "A man like him could lead me to salvation with the Master... as his wife."

"It seems that you've submitted to humility," he noted. "Deacon and I have decided that you are to be a second wife to Elder Morris when he gets his position on the counsel."

I felt faint. "I'm sorry, Elder," I blurted out. "I was wrong. I'm not ready!"

"Nonsense," Elder Chatson replied. "The elders all believe you are ready to serve the community as a wife. Tomorrow, you'll help Goodwife Morris serve him and his son dinner. The marriage ceremony will be on the Sabbath after your next cycle. We'll send you for your last exam tomorrow and then the Handmaiden House will start your preparation."

My knees almost buckled under me.

"You're dismissed, Suzannah."

CHAPTER 15

I wanted to run to the Maarses' quarters, but I realized they would not be there. It was time for worship. They would be in the worship hall with everyone else in the commune. Everyone had gathered already and Deacon was at the pulpit by the time I arrived. He paused when I tried to sneak in the back of the chapel. Everyone turned to stare at me.

My mother was sitting with my siblings in the back of the room. "Suzannah," she hissed, grabbing my sleeve. I slipped into the bench beside her. Goody Maars glanced back at me, but Mother grabbed my elbow and pulled me close to her.

"You don't know what a relief it is to know you're getting married to an Elder," she whispered in my ear. "I thought you'd age out of the Handmaiden House after that stunt in the Maarses' quarters. You'll come back to our quarters after this, understand?"

I did understand. This meant I was going to be punished by her. Anger welled up behind my eyes. For three months she's treated me like I didn't exist. Now I'm her daughter again, to punish as she sees fit?

"And tonight, as we go towards our beds prayerfully, I must announce something the Great Master is bestowing on us. We must rejoice, He told me early this morning that a match was to be made: Elder Morris is to take a second wife. The wife that the Great Master is giving to him is… Suzannah Commons. She has served her punishment for sinning, and she is ready to become a wife. Suzannah, will you join us here on the altar to accept the proposal, despite how you disturbed our worship earlier?"

I knew it wasn't a question, or an invitation. It was a command. I swallowed the bile that had risen in my throat, stood. Mother released my arm, but the grimace never left her face. I smoothed my blouse and skirt, and set out on the journey to the altar, where Deacon was waiting with his Elders and Sub-Elders. My heart thundered with every step. Everyone turned to stare at me.

My legs trembled as I ascended the steps to the altar.

Deacon extended his hand and placed it on my shoulder. "Kneel," he instructed, guiding me to my place before Morris.

I bowed my head.

"Repeat after me, Suzannah: Do you take me under your wing as a wife, to guide me, to make sure I do not sin, that I shall multiply your children, like fruits on the vine?"

I swallowed hard. Spots swirled in front of my eyes. "Do you take me under your wing as a wife, to guide me, to make sure I do not sin, that I shall multiply your children, like fruits on the vine?" I repeated.

Morris placed a hand atop my head. "I shall."

"The engagement ceremony is complete. We shall begin Suzannah's preparation to become one of Morris' wives. Can we give Elder Morris a round of congratulatory applause?"

There was a smattering of applause: I had grown up seeing this ceremony, but usually it was more enthusiastic. The girls from the Handmaidens House looked like they had bitten into a sour persimmon, as if I had personally offended them. There was a fury on Simber's face, but Oakley was clapping loudly and grinning widely. She seemed genuinely excited for me.

"Suzannah?" Deacon harrumphed, as if I had forgotten something. He was holding out his hand with the ring. I kissed it. Then I had to kiss Morris's left ring finger as well, as a sign of our engagement.

"You are dismissed. As it should be."

"As it should be," the congregation replied.

By the time I regained my feet Morris had already left the platform. It was as if I were already forgotten and of no consequence. I tried to slip unnoticed off the altar, but Oakley ran up and hugged me.

"I'm so excited that you've been promised!" she cried, glowing for me, then she stopped and gazed into my eyes. "Why don't you look happy?"

In Oakley's version of life in Home I certain should be happy. It was every handmaiden's dream, to marry an elder, to avoid aging out and being sent to the Hard Labor camp.

But I no longer lived in Oakley's world. I didn't want Morris. Or any other elder. I wanted... I wanted *Silas.* But how could I tell her that?

I saw Silas, trying to get through the throng, but Mother was ahead of him. She grabbed my arm and dragged me out of the worship hall, furious.

"You're lucky you got promised," she snarled in a low whisper.

"But what have I done-"

"I don't want to hear it!" she spat. She shoved me into

her quarters, spun me around and slapped me hard across the face. "Why did you burst into the worship hall right after you were told you were to be a wife to Elder Morris? Why did you do that?"

I was speechless.

"Lift up your skirt."

My sores from the lashing Deacon gave me had barely healed. Goody had taken the stitches out just yesterday.

"Now, Suzannah!"

Something snapped inside me. In less than a month I was to be an Elder's wife. I would rank higher than she in the eyes of the community. I would not submit to this! I stood up straight, pushed my shoulders back and met her furious stare with one of my own.

"No."

The look on my mother's face was so comical I almost laughed out loud.

"Girl, you didn't just reject me," she snarled, and grabbed my hair.

I shrieked, and she twisted her fist in my hair, pulling my head down. I struggled back against her, and swung at her, but she smacked me back, on my rear end. I took a swing at her, not willing to give in and allow her to beat me. I kicked at her, connecting my boot against her thigh. She gasped in pain and let go of my hair. I retreated to the wall. Her eyes were so wide, I thought she'd snap. She groaned, and stroked the spot on her thigh where I had kicked her.

"Suzannah," she breathed. "How could you kick me?" she asked, as if I had been the one that attacked her first.

I kicked you because you had no right or reason to hit me, I thought bitterly. As I opened my mouth to respond, there came a knock on the door, followed a voice.

"Goody Commons?"

It was Goody Maars. "Did Suzannah come back here with you? We just received word that she will no longer be serving us, but I need her for one more night." She opened the door and stepped inside. Her voice was oddly cold. "Ephraim's been having headaches; I must tend to him, but there are services that need to be performed in the infirmary. I need Suzannah's assistance one last time."

"Use her however you like," my mother seethed. "She is no daughter of mine."

"Suzannah, you will come with me," Goody Maars said, extending a hand. Her voice was cold as she spoke. She grabbed my elbow roughly and pulled me away from my mother. My younger siblings were waiting outside the door. My father was walking toward the quarters.

"Goodwife, where are you taking my daughter?" Papa said.

"She's being disciplined," Goody Maars snapped. "As I understand it, you have no daughter. We'll take care of it."

She yanked me away from him. A sense of dread washed over me. I had trusted Goodwife Maars! Why had she turned on me? Was she going to whip me, too?

"Goody Maars…"

"Hush, child!" she said. "Stars! Don't say a word."

She didn't say anything else until we got to her quarters.

"Ephraim!" she shouted. "Turn on the white noise machines *now*."

Dr. Maars flipped on the machines and the rooms were flooded with sound.

"I'm sorry I handled you that way in the hall, but I had to," Goody Maars said. "We can't afford to appear sympathetic to your fear of being married. But I understand it."

I snorted and sobbed in response. She dabbed at my runny nose.

"I'll leave you two alone," Dr. Maars said.

She squeezed my hand. "Do you need anything?"

I shook my head, but saw a tear drip down my nose.

"I don't want to be married to Morris," I said.

"I wish I could do something," she said. "But when the Elders agree that a girl is ready for marriage…"

"I'm not ready to be a wife," I whispered.

"Deacon thinks you are. Deacon thinks marrying girls off young keeps them from having time to think too much, that having babies will be all the distraction you need to stop being so subversive to his cause."

"What does that mean?"

"Someone who subverts the system… *undermines* it."

"And that's what I am?"

"Yes. You're getting ideas. I don't know, maybe it's my fault. I just saw a spark in you, a sweetness that I didn't want to see snuffed out, an eagerness to learn. I didn't want to see you turned into an overworked wife with ten children underfoot and three in the grave. Maybe that's why I treated you as if you were my own daughter like this. In Deacon's eyes, I'm wrong."

"But do *you* think you're wrong?"

She shook her head.

"No. I'm not wrong. I can't be. I can't *afford* to be."

I laid my head against her shoulder and she stroked my hair. I didn't want to be a wife. Not yet. Certainly not to Elder Morris. But I didn't want to be sent to the Hard Labor camp, either.

"Goody Maars," I sniffed. "Would you consider yourself subversive?"

She was silent for a long moment, and a wry smile turned up the corners of her mouth. "Yes, Suzannah," she said. "I suppose I am."

I nodded. I'd miss the books. I'd miss the stories. And I'd miss my family. It was odd to think of the Maarses as my family, but I did.

"Ephraim," Goody Maars called out. Dr. Maars stuck his head through the door. "Can you ask the Elders to wait on her marriage?"

"No," he said.

"Ephraim!"

"Marissa, don't put me in this position!"

I squeezed Goody Maars' hand and exhaled.

There was a long silence.

"Don't put *Suzannah* in this position," she said. "You can speak for her. I can't."

He exhaled loudly. "Fine. I can't guarantee they'll listen to me."

"Thank you," I said. "Thank you, Dr. Maars."

"Gather your things, now dear," Goody said. "You must go back to the Handmaiden House."

I nodded. I walked back to the boys' room to retrieve the laundry sack. Silas shut the door behind me. Anger, hurt, and emotions I couldn't put a name to etched his face.

"Silas," I whispered.

"Suzannah, I'm so sorry," he breathed. His arms slipped around me and my heart began to pound. That now familiar longing for him, the excitement of that first kiss, welled up inside me. I was shaking. He kissed me, his mouth hot and urgent on mine. I kissed him back, more frantic than in the Ruins. He pushed me back and held me at arm's length. "I'm going to the Elders. I'm going to put in a petition to marry you."

"You can't," I protested. "I'm already promised to Elder Morris!"

"I don't care," he said, his eyes flamed. "I don't want Morris to have you. I don't want anyone else to have you. Do you want anybody else to have you?"

I shook my head. "I only want you."

Tears welled up in my eyes. I had only a vague understanding of the mechanics of the wedding night, but I knew I didn't want that to happen with Elder Morris. I wanted to preserve that private part of my body for myself, not have it taken from me against my will. I wanted to give that experience to Silas. I knew he'd be careful with me. He wouldn't hurt me and he wouldn't scare me.

"I want to leave, Silas," I whispered. "Can we leave together?"

"I want to. With you. So badly." He kissed me again, our breath ragged, the air in the room suddenly too hot. I slipped my arms around him and squeezed him close to me. I kissed him. I held him as if I were holding onto my sanity. I held him as if he were my only hope. He was all those things for me.

In that small moment, as the tears slipped down my face, I realized two things: I truly loved Silas and we were destined to be separated.

"We can run away together," he whispered. "We'll go to the Ruins and wait for the Americans. I'll take you away. I promise."

✦ ✦ ✦

Goody Maars walked me to Elder Morris's quarters in the late night. "Keep your eyes down," she admonished as she knocked on the door.

The door opened. I saw Elder Morris's shoes appear.

"Why did it take so long to bring her to me, Goody Maars?" Morris asked.

"She required a whipping for her behavior at worship from her mother," Goody said. "Ephraim isn't feeling well, so I interrupted Goody Commons and ended up having to lash her a few more times myself. But she's learned her lesson. That's what kept her so long with us. Ephraim sends his apologies."

"Duly noted," Morris said. "All I require is for her to gather our laundry. She can clean the quarters more thoroughly tomorrow." He reached toward me, and I felt him lift a stray lock of my hair with one of his fingers and twirl it. Revulsion coursed through my veins at his touch.

"I've grown accustomed to her taking over most of my responsibilities," she said. Goody Maars shoved me into the quarters. "I'll miss her strong back. You could say her presence has left me a bit spoiled."

"Goodnight, Goodwife Maars," Morris said. "I'll be sitting at my own table tomorrow, but I'll make sure Suzannah serves breakfast for your family, too. I know your husband gives you other work duties to complete."

"Goodnight, Elder. As it should be."

The door shut.

Cassandra walked in with her baby in her arms. She regarded me coldly and pointed to the laundry sack in the corner. "Take this," she snapped. "And get out of my sight."

I picked up the laundry sack and left without another word. While crossing the courtyard to the Handmaiden House I paused to look up to the main building of the compound. I saw Silas's outline in his quarters. He was watching me.

He had cried, something men don't do, when talking

about me tonight, when he kissed me. Silas cried for *me*.

The thought brought tears to my own eyes; tears of joy, and tears of fear. For Silas to cry like he did… I realized his feelings for me had to be intense. Did he love me the way I loved him?

For the time being, there was nothing I could do except hope that he did.

CHAPTER 16

Istumbled into the Handmaiden House with the laundry sacks from the Maarses' and the Morrises' quarters, completely dazed at my realization.

Silas.

His name sounded holy and reverential; like a prayer. My hope. I shivered at the thought of him.

As I undressed and put on my nightclothes. Simber and Oakley were waiting on their beds. They hadn't spoken to me in weeks.

"Well, aren't you the lucky one?" Simber sneered. "Already engaged, despite sinning so badly."

"It's exciting that Elder Morris wants you to be his wife," Oakley countered, her face aglow with excitement. "Just think; soon you'll be out of the Handmaiden House and start having babies! Isn't that wonderful?"

I regarded both Simber and Oakley with equal reserve. I thought about what Silas had said to me; about how Dr. Maars treated Goody Maars; about Jane Eyre and how she hadn't settled for being some human possession in her husband's eyes. She had been an equal. I want to be my husband's equal, like the doctor and the goodwife; to experience the love they had and to feel what I felt when I was alone with Silas, kissing him, and not be afraid of indulging in it.

"Suzannah?" Oakley asked. "What's wrong?"

I shook my head. Simber, Oakley, the other girls in the Handmaiden House…none of them had the slightest notion of what might be possible for them; for all of us.

"I don't want that," I said. I didn't mean to say it out loud, but once the words started, I couldn't stop myself. "I don't want to be someone's wife if we don't have love."

"Of course he'll love you," Oakley chattered on. "We love everyone in this commune. Except for the labor whores. They've undermined everything Deacon does to save us for the Master."

"As if they've done anything wrong," I shot back. "Those girls were put in the Hard Labor camp because Deacon believes they might dare to think for themselves."

Their jaws dropped in disgust.

"You don't want to be one of them, do you?" Simber asked, horrified.

"No, I don't want to be one of them. But I don't want to be married to an old man who doesn't care about me, either. Besides, Silas likes me," I said. "Silas is putting in a petition to marry me."

Simber laughed snidely. "Oh, the great Suzannah Commons has two men pursuing her to make her their wife. We should all be so lucky."

"Simber," Oakley admonished before turning her attention to me. "Suzannah, just think," she said. "If it hadn't been for us telling the truth to the Elders, you'd never be coveted as a wife by two men. Isn't it exciting?"

Her words hit me as if I had run into a wall.

I felt sick.

"You told the Elders what truth?" But I already knew.

"That you saw Silas naked," Oakley said. "See how everything worked out?"

I felt like I had taken a fist to my stomach, as the realization set in. Oakley and Simber betrayed me! It wasn't Silas. All this time, I had blamed Silas for my punishment. I wronged him. How could I have been so stupid? How could I have trusted Oakley and Simber?

I hated them. I had never really and truly hated anyone before, but at that moment, I realized what hate was. I laid down on my bed and rolled over with my back to them.

"I don't know why you're not happy," Simber said, running a brush through her long, unbraided hair. "You're getting married. That *should* make you happy. Instead, you're pouting and upset. All the girls dream of getting married to an Elder. I don't know what you're so upset about."

I laid down in bed, my tears leaking onto the pillow.

I walked into the infirmary to see Goody Maars. The infirmary wasn't filled up with people today. I took it as a good sign.

The last few days had involved cooking and cleaning for Morris, although he never spoke directly to me. Mostly I assisted Cassandra with their ill-behaved, three-year-old son, Jason, fed the children and put them to bed.

Last night was different. I was busy shoving a pile of soiled clothing from the nursery into the laundry sack when Morris walked up behind me.

"Suzannah?"

I straightened up and lowered my eyes.

I kept my back to him. "Yes, sir?"

"I want to talk to you. You will sit down at the table with me," he said. "Come this way."

I followed him to the table and he pulled out a chair. I waited for him to sit first.

"Please," he said, pulling out the chair for me.

I was surprised, and more than a bit apprehensive. He had never done this for me; no man ever had, asides from Silas and Dr. Maars. I had never seen him do this for Cassandra. I knew from the stories Dr. Maars read that at one time it was a common practice for men to pull chairs out for women. It was considered proper courtesy and good manners.

They didn't any longer. Today such an action would be considered a weakness in a man. *What is he up to?* I wondered. *Why is he being nice to me? Is he trying to get me to like him?*

I sat, then he sat down beside me.

"Suzannah, do you want to be my wife?" he asked.

It was a dangerous question; one I wanted desperately to answer correctly. A wrong answer would not have pleasant repercussions.

"If Deacon believes this is best, then this is best for me," I lied.

Morris reached over and put a hand on my knee. Revulsion shot through my body and I tried to not squirm away from his touch. He squeezed my knee.

"I've had my eye on you for a while. You're plain enough, but you are not completely unattractive, and you are, for the most part, obedient. But Suzannah, you do have a wild side. You understand that, don't you?"

His hand slid further up my thigh. An uncomfortable whimper slipped out of my mouth.

"My job as a husband is to quell that wild side and make you a daughter for the Master."

He leaned close to me, his breath hot against my neck, and whispered into my ear, "Now, Suzannah, you seem to have some silly notion about love." His breath stank and I wanted to turn my face away, but I didn't dare. "I don't think you know what true love is. I wish you did. The Master instructs men to show women the way to the light, to offer them hope when they don't even know what hope is."

Morris sniffed my hair. I bit my tongue to keep from crying out.

"There appears to be some competition for your heart," he chuckled, as if it were of no consequence. "I shouldn't have to compete with a child like Silas, a mere boy is unfit for husbandhood, one who has never even sampled a woman."

His hand slipped to the inside of my thigh and he pushed it further up. I understood with horror that he had no intention of stopping. Bile rose in my throat. His hand suddenly tightened and he wrapped his other arm around my waist.

"I want you to listen to me carefully, Suzannah," he continued to speak as if he were a sage and I was an eager student. "You will be my wife, or you won't. But you will never be Silas's wife. It is only my protection that is keeping you from being sentenced to the hard labor camp.

"You don't truly think that your punishment has actually atoned for your sins, do you? No, no, no. Your heart is desperately wicked; I know the sinful and lustful thoughts you have for Silas Maars. You can only be saved through childbearing; if not in an honorable marriage to me, then through the ignoble services you will perform in the Hard Labor camps, where the militia boys come at night to punish those whores for their disobedience.

"Those girls inevitably become pregnant, but they must expect no reprieve from their work. The conditions are harsh and if the pregnancy comes to term, the babies die. The mothers, too. They all die; their bodies dumped into a mass grave behind the commune; no names, no markers, no nothing. They're gone. Forgotten forever. Even the Great Master turns His back on them. In the afterlife, they're doomed to spend eternity in the great pit of fire."

He paused, letting his words worm their way into my mind, his fingers caressing my inner thigh. Suddenly he thrust his hand up legs to my groin. I gasped in horror. I almost retched. I wasn't even allowed to touch that part of myself. I was reserved for my husband. Deacon said so! Yet this Elder was brazenly touching it. I struggled to move away, but he held me fast, squeezed me to him.

"You don't want to spend your life in the Hard Labor camp and eternity in the pit of fire, do you?"

I grasped his hand arm and pulled on it, trying to get his hand off from there. I couldn't move him. "No!" I sobbed. "No! Stop, please, let go of me!"

"Suzannah," he said. "Be my wife. Let the Maars boy know that you have no interest in him. His time will come, eventually. In the meantime, I will get his excess energy out by taking him to the labor camp, unless he's as queer as they say. Do we understand each other?"

I looked into his face. I instantly regretted it. His eyes were wild, droplets of sweat fell from his upper lip, and a hint of a wicked smile tugged at the corners of his lips. He's enjoying this, I thought, tears streaming down my cheeks.

"Yes, sir," I uttered.

As if I had said the magic words, Morris released me, pulled his hand from between my legs, stood and walked away. He stopped, almost as an afterthought, and turned back to me.

"You will be mine shortly. And if you don't bleed..." He left the rest unsaid.

I ran back to the Handmaiden House that night and buried my face in my pillow to keep anyone from hearing my sobs. Not that anyone there would care. I was ashamed, humiliated, embarrassed by Morris' handling of my body. The events replayed over and over in my mind and I couldn't stop them. I felt dirty. I had caused this.

"Suzannah?" Goody Maars stood in the doorway. Her voice jarred me back to the present.

"Hello," I whispered.

"You look sick. Is everything okay?"

I shook my head.

She took my arm and guided me into Dr. Maars' office. I sat on the examination table.

"Did something happen, Suzannah?"

I drew in a deep breath and blew it out. I tried to tell her about Morris touching me, but I couldn't force the words out of my mouth. Instead, I told her about his ultimatum. "He told me that if I didn't become his wife, I'd be sent to the Hard Labor camp."

"That's not true," Goody Maars tried to comfort me. "Morris does not have the authority to sentence anyone to the Hard Labor camp. Not on his own, anyway. Young women stay in the Handmaiden House until they marry or age out. That is the law."

"He told me to tell Silas to stop pursuing me."

She sighed. "Silas did petition the council for permission to marry you," she admitted.

"It was unwise; we told him not to."

I sucked in a ragged breath. I wanted so badly to tell her what Morris had done to me, how ashamed and scared it made me feel, and to have her tell me that what he did was wrong. But I was afraid she wouldn't be so understanding; that she would say I had tempted Morris, that I was in the wrong. I hadn't meant to cause anything, but I inevitiably did.

Confusion jumbled my thoughts. What if my purity was completely compromised? Could Dr. Maars or Goody save me if it came out that Morris had touched me because I tempted him? I honestly don't know what I did to tempt him. *How can I not to tempt a man? Was my body, my very existience all that men needed to lose control?*

Tears blurred my eyes. The events played out in my mind all over again. I was all my fault! *I'm dirty for tempting him. He knew I had lustful thoughts about Silas, and I still imagined him naked before I fell asleep at night. How did he know that?*

"Suzannah?" I heard Goody distantly. "Suzannah!"

I stared at her for a long moment, then dropped my eyes to my hands. "I'm scared," I whispered. "I'm so scared, Goody."

"I know," she stroked my hair. "For young girls, the thought of marriage can be terrifying; especially your first night alone with your husband. I want you to be prepared, but the Elders don't care if you are or not." A hard look veiled Goody's eyes. "I'm sending a message to the Elders that you aren't well and need more time before the marriage is put in place." She took my hand. "Suzannah? Whatever happens, even if you do get sentenced to the Hard Labor camp, we'll come and get you. And leave. I won't stand for it. I promise you that."

I looked into her face. Tears lined her eyes.

"I love you. Very much."

I didn't see Goody or any of the Maarses for the next few days. I was squeamish and scared when I walked into the Morris quarters, afraid of being alone with Elder Morris, but Cassandra was always around. Even though she hated me, she served as my protector without even realizing it.

At night, I stayed in the Handmaiden House. I was lonely. Without Simber and Oakley, I had no friends left; no one to talk to.

My cycle came, and I was afraid. The terms of my betrothal were the marriage would take place following my cycle. I had spent the time before bed praying my cycle would never come again. The Handmaiden House Matron reported it to Deacon. Now I wished this cycle would last forever, even during the pain.

Having your cycle did not relieve you of your duties. I performed my chores as always. I served Morris his midday meal, staring longingly at his portions. Goody Morris rarely left much for me to eat, and I was so very hungry.

The laundry was hot, the late-summer air muggy and close. I tied my hair back from my face and started on the Morris family's laundry. Once I finished their laundry, I could start on my regular laundry chores. I went through my tasks like one of the reanimated dead. My flow of blood had stopped. I bit my lip and tried not to think about what that meant.

The Laundry Matron stopped in front of me.

"Yes, Matron?" I curtsied.

"You've been summoned to Deacon's personal meeting room," she said, her hands on her hips. She did not look happy to be deprived of a worker, even for a summons from Deacon. "The others can split up the rest of your quota."

The Elders' wing was busy, with clerks and assistants and Sub-Elders moving between the offices, handling the daily administration of the commune. I knocked on the door to the office and waited. *Why am I here? What have I done wrong this time? Am I to meet the Elders?*

As I waited, my thoughts drifted back to my impending wedding. *Would I be prepared by my sisters in the Handmaiden House for marriage? Would any of them even be willing to touch me?*

The door finally opened. There were only two men in Deacon's meeting room; Deacon and Morris.

"Hello, Suzannah," Deacon said. I lowered my eyes to the floor. "Do you know why we called you?"

"No, sir," I said, shaking my head.

"We know that you were lashed on the evening of your betrothal to Elder Morris."

I nodded, embarrassment creeping up my cheeks. "Yes, sir, that is correct."

"I've received messages From Dr. Maars that you need more time to heal before you can perform the duties of a goodwife."

I waited. I wasn't sure if there was some question in his statement that I needed to answer. I said nothing.

"You are afraid of becoming a wife," he continued. "I understand that. Most girls are scared of what becoming a wife entails. It is, after all, a world of experiences that can only properly and spiritually be taught to them through union with a proper husband; one who is assigned by me, of course.

"I get the impression that you've grown quite close to Goodwife Maars and her family. I also have the feeling that young Silas Maars thinks he has the proper amount of life experiences to husband you."

Deacon stood, walked across the room, and circled me slowly. I felt as if his eyes were measuring me, weighing me, finding all the flaws in me. A dark chill ran down my spine. As if satisfied by his examination, Deacon strode back to his desk and sat down. He leaned forward and propped his chin on his hands.

"I assure you, Suzannah," the Maars lad does not have the knowledge or experience to govern himself, much less guide a woman in the holy ways. I'm sure by now you know that Dr. Maars is seeking dispensation on his son's behalf for you. Will you admit to being aware of them? Remember, omission is a sin."

I bit my lip, striving to keep my eyes fixed on the floor. "Yes, sir, I know. Silas liked me acting as a wife would before his family."

Deacon nodded, apparently pleased with my answer.

"Perhaps you know that I am responsible for Ephraim's marriage to Marissa. She wouldn't look at him twice, but he noticed her. She was not pleased when I announced their match, but I knew the will of the Great Master. They are well matched, don't you think?"

That's not what they told me, I thought.

"Yes, Deacon. They are well matched," I answered.

"You may not know that I have given Ephraim, Dr. Maars, more than adequate opportunities to take a second wife."

Morris walked behind me and placed his hand on my shoulder. He began to squeeze. I shivered, wanting to wriggle away. This felt wrong. It was wrong, but I couldn't pull away from him. I feared I'd lose whatever favor I had just gained with Deacon if I did. He continued. "He has always declined the offer, stating that he has too much to do; that he doesn't have the time to devote to spiritually guide another wife," Deacon continued. "I must admit, with a commune this large, the needs of the whole certainly outweigh needs of the individual, so I've made an exception on Ephraim's behalf. I would like to elevate Ephraim to the status of Elder. We could use his wisdom the Elder's council. But he insists his work is increasing and he has no time for such an honor."

Deacon paused for a moment. Morris crossed back to his chair beside Deacon's desk and sat.

"Ephraim wants to train you to assist his wife in the infirmary as the commune's next midwife."

I dared to raise my eyes at this. Was it possible? My heart leapt at the thought.

"I told him that until you have a child of your own, you have no business watching other women give birth. That's not for virgin eyes."

I bit my lip to keep from weeping. My hopes were crushed. I should have expected this.

"Now, Suzannah, do you have any questions at this point?"

"Yes, sir, I do."

"You may ask."

I gulped, seeing Morris's feet. "What about Silas's request for my hand in marriage?"

Deacon let out a deep sigh as if all his work to instruct a dimwitted child had been to no avail. He stood and walked toward me, stopping in front of me.

"There are requests which are blessed by the Great Master, and there are requests which are not in His will," Deacon said. "You are needed as Elder Morris's wife. The Great Master told me so."

A hand glided under my chin. I flinched. Deacon

gripped my face roughly and lifted my chin. "Look me in the eyes, girl."

I did. Deacon's eyes horrified me. There was a sickly green-red tinge that colored his pupils and dull yellow film that coated the whites of his eyes wasn't natural. How could the entire commune miss the fact that Deacon is so ill? His breath smelled like rotting meat; worse than Morris's.

"You women are delicate and pretty to look at," he declared, "but inside you are weak and infirm. You are prone to depression; you become unhinged, unstable. You damage your souls and tempt men to sinful thoughts and actions. This is why I betrothed you to Elder Morris. Can you not see I am doing this for your good? You are loved by the Great Master, but only when you are controlled properly." He released my jaw and I immediately focused my eyes to the floor, away from his awful jaundiced eyes. "Tell the truth; have you finished your cycle?"

I took a deep breath and bit my lip.

"Don't even think about lying to me, girl. I have reports. I'll you examine you myself if I have to."

The thought alone was enough to make me feel ill. I took a deep breath. "Yes. My cycle is past."

He nodded and stepped to the side. ""Bend over. Put your hands on my desk."

I hesitated.

"I will not ask you twice."

I obeyed. I knew Deacon was a liar, but I also knew he wasn't lying about that statement.

"Please…"

"Suzannah, do not question," Morris said.

"Deacon, are you going to whip me again?" I asked, not caring what Morris was commanding.

I was terrified. Haven't I been whipped enough lately? My legs can't stand another session of stitches.

"No," Deacon said. "I'm not going to whip you. But I have the feeling the Maarses have been less than truthful about your health."

Shaking, I lowered my face so that the tip of my nose touched the desktop. I could see indentations in the wood from pen tips, a few ink splotches, and a chip in the varnish. My whole body shook.

"Lift up her skirt, Elder."

My knees were shaking so hard, I thought my legs would buckle under me. I felt my skirt being lifted, exposing the back of my legs, without a thought for any embarrassment I might feel.

"They lied," Morris crowed, victorious inquest. "She's healed up just fine. They've taken the stitches out and her bruises have completely faded."

Deacon sighed. "I suppose they were trying to delay the inevitable."

"I want them punished," Morris demanded.

"They are only acting as any concerned parents would. They think of Suzannah as their own."

"Don't I get a say in who I marry?" I blurted out. "Silas wants me. He wants to be the next doctor of Home, and he wants me to work with him as the next midwife." I knew I was making the biggest mistake of my life, but I couldn't stop the words from pouring out of my mouth. "Elder Morris, I'll continue to work for you. I'll work harder than I have. Please, I'm only asking for the chance to choose."

The two men stood dumbfounded. I wasn't sure if any woman had ever has asked them for a choice before. Emboldened by their silence, I pressed forward with my argument.

"Think about what might happen if Dr. Maars get hurt or fall ill? Home must have a trained physician. Please, Deacon, I beg you. Let me marry Silas. I'll continue to serve Elder Morris as his housekeeper..."

"You will not make a fool of me," Morris roared. He turned to Deacon, rage painting his face. He shook his finger at me. "She's insubordinate and disobedient..."

"Yes," Deacon said. "She is."

If I had believed Deacon had a benevolent bone in his body, that belief was now squashed.

He grabbed my wrists hard and shoved me toward Morris. "This is my command. Take her now. Give her the choice and time to consider: Hard Labor camp or your bed. She will be in one or the other within the fortnight."

Morris grabbed my arms and spun me around, forcing me face down on Deacon's desk. I struggled to pull away, but Morris held me down with one hand. My skirts flew up over my hips and I could feel Morris's hand yanking down my undergarments.

"Stop!" I screamed, knowing that everyone else was in the Great Hall, that no one would hear my cries. My nails dug into the desktop. "Deacon, make it stop!"

Morris wrapped his free arm around my waist; I felt his rotting breath against my ear, I could smell it.

"I warned you, girl," Morris snarled in my ear. He kicked his feet between mine, forcing them apart. I tried to clamp my legs together.

"I won't make this easy or nice for you."

I had known pain before, but nothing like this, not this long-standing, knee-bucklingly bad, like liquid pain pouring in the most private part of me. My screams caught in my throat. I started to collapse, but Morris held me up so he could continue. Something trickling down my thighs, something sticky, warm, and thick. It had to be blood. I squirmed, trying to push away.

Stars above, when will this end? I was shaking.

"Stop!" I cried out. "Please?" Pleading was of no use.

"Stop moving," Morris snapped. He grabbed my hair and pulled. "Or I will make it worse."

I wanted to die. This was what women experienced on their marriage nights? No wonder mothers didn't talk to their daughters about it.

The smell of blood hit my nostrils, along with something unfamiliar. I didn't want this!

If this was the end result of exploring my future with Silas, I was a fool. I had to be daft. I couldn't imagine why I let this thought pervade my mind.

Maybe the Maarses really were deviants. Maybe I wasn't meant to be equal to my husband. How had I been so foolish?

Morris finally stopped. He stepped away from me, breathing heavy. I lay over Deacon's desk, whimpering and quivering. I reached down and pulled my undergarments up, then collapsed on the floor.

"Suzannah," Deacon intoned, his voice deep, resonate, so reasonable. "You now understand what the girls in the Hard Labor camps experience every night. When you came into my office, you seemed averse to being Elder Morris's second wife. I believe that aversion was based in some youthful misconception.

"We are not savages, Suzannah. We won't force any woman to marry against her will. You have the option to reject Elder Morris as your husband. Of course, by rejecting Elder Morris you are choosing to enter the Hard Labor camp, which would validate your position in the commune as a whore since you are obviously no longer a virgin.

"In my great love and mercy, I'm going to give you another day to reconsider. You asked for the chance to choose. Very well, you get to make your own choice. But you are as worthless as you are stupid if you don't choose to marry Elder Morris."

CHAPTER 17

I huddled on the floor of the tiny room, shivering from fear and shock. There was no cot or bed, no heat, no water, not even a slop bucket. There was one door, which was locked and barred from the outside, and one window, which was crisscrossed with heavy iron bars. I watched the sun set through those bars. I would scream, but there was no one near enough to hear. This punishment room was situated on the outskirts of the commune, far away from any community activity, far enough away that the members of the commune wouldn't be disturbed by they cries of a prisoner who was going slowly insane from hunger, thirst and exposure.

The scene played out over and over again in my mind. I couldn't think. I couldn't move. I could feel the blood trickling down my inner thighs. It had nothing to do with my cycle. I bent over and retched on the floor, wiped my mouth on my sleeve, then fixed my eyes back on the setting sun.

Twenty-four hours.

The thought emerged, unbidden, in my mind.

Twenty-four hours to decide my own fate. Would I be better off married to a despicable old man who raped me; or be a whore in the Hard Labor camp, ravaged by random soldiers every night?

Logic said marriage to Morris was less traumatic. *I'd rather be dead!* I wanted to marry Silas, but I was damaged, useless, nothing. There was no way I'd be acceptable as a wife to Silas now. I was completely destitute.

The sun disappeared beyond the horizon, and the moon appeared, at least until an ominous thundercloud rolled in, rumbling angrily as if in protest against the injustice of Home.

Where will I be tomorrow night? In the infirmary? In the Morris private quarters? In the Hard Labor camp? In the graveyard behind the commune? On a pyre? A cockroach crawled across my shoe. I half-heartedly kicked it away. It scurried into a crack in the tiles. A few other cockroaches in the corner regarded me, as if scared of me.

Second star to the right, straight on 'til morning.

Why would those cockroaches be afraid of me? I am nothing; just a weak little girl, scared, injured, broken. My virginity, the only thing of value that had ever belonged to me, was gone.

I don't remember sleeping, but I must have. I was afraid my dreams would be haunted by the events of the day. Instead, my dreams were of the times I had spent with the Maars family, the trip to the Ruins, the evenings listening to Dr. Maars read. I awoke to the thought; *I'll never see the Alley or the Ruins again. I'll never hold Telly again, or see Noah's drawings.* A shudder racked my body. I'll never get to kiss Silas again. My heart broke as I thought about losing Silas, his kisses, the fire in my stomach. Tears leaked down my cheeks. *I'll never be with him again.*

The sun began to rise. I started to stand, but the pain was enormous. Why are we even alive if this is fate as women? I wondered. I began to understand why my mother was such a bitter, hateful woman. I can't live this way. I shook my head. I'd rather be dead.

Goody Maars' words hit me.

We'll never leave without you.

It was the one thought that made sense to me. This is how she survives: her love for her children, for her husband. And she loves me! I envisioned her kind, sad eyes, viewing me; her soft, weathered smile; her peace-evoking voice. I love you. The thought banished the events from the night from my mind. How could she love a girl who had been so stupid as to plead for a choice from Deacon, only to have her virginity ripped from her, like a fool?

The early morning wake-up bell shrieked. I was famished. And thirsty. I hadn't eaten since yesterday's breakfast. I wasn't sure I could survive this, but I determined to try.

I heard the militia training outside the window, the sergeant barking numbers and the sound of their boots against the ground. The events of the previous day began to play in my head again.

No, no, no, no, stop! I forced the vision from my mind.

My stomach growled. I ignored it. My tongue swelled. I ignored it. I felt the warmth of the sun on my flesh. I refused to acknowledge it. I felt dead inside. All that was left for me was to be dead on the outside, too.

It was coming soon enough. They would come and ask for my decision in front of the whole commune; as if it were really a decision.

I allowed myself a wry smile imagining the look on their faces when I announced my choice. I'd choose neither; I'd ask them to kill me.

I wanted to meet God; not this Great Master deity that Deacon had made up. No, I wanted to meet the God that Silas and Goody Maars talked about, the one from the Holy Book, the one that Deacon was defacing. I wanted to meet all three of Them.

There was a knock on my door and a familiar voice, but not the voice I expected.

"Suzannah?"

The voice had a higher pitch than Morris and Deacon. "Suzannah, are you in here?"

"Silas?" I croaked, my lips cracked from thirst. It was Silas. My Silas, with his beautiful heart and his kind, forgiving soul. My heart broke into a thousand shards. There was no happily ever after for us.

I crawled to the door on my hands and knees, begging, weeping. "Silas, get me out of here! Please!" I sobbed. I knew it was impossible. "Unlock the door!"

"Lay down on the floor, as far away from the door as you can," he commanded.

"Okay," I gasped between the sobs.

"Cover your head, and plug your ears."

I curled back up into the corner, covering my head with my hands.

There was a loud bang. I could hear nothing except a loud ringing. I think I screamed, but I couldn't even hear myself. When I dared to look back, there was a hole in the door where the doorknob used to be. The door creaked open and hung on its lopsided on its hinges. Silas stood there, his rifle in his hands, looking like the wrath of God.

He ran into the room and wrapped me up in his arms.

"I'm so sorry," he said over and over, somehow his words penetrated the incessant ringing in my ears. "I was supposed to protect you. I'm so sorry!"

"Silas!" I sobbed into his chest. "I tried, I said it wrong and…"

"I'm taking you away from here. Tonight."

I lifted my head. "Why?"

"Stop asking why," he commanded. "We have to go, now."

"Silas, I'm dirty." I pleaded. "You shouldn't even be touching me…"

"We can talk about it later," he said. "Come on." We turned to leave the little room, but a figure blocked the doorway.

"I tried to be merciful, but it seems you'd prefer to join the other whores in the Hard Labor camp," Deacon said. He stood there, his eyes narrow, a shiny silver pair of shears in his hand.

Silas lifted his rifle and pointed it at Deacon's chest. "You should step aside, Deacon," he said. "I'm taking Suzannah and we're leaving the commune as husband and wife."

"She's not fit to be a wife, Silas," Deacon smiled. "She has been defiled and ruined. I orderd it, and I watched it-"

"Because of the respect my father has for you, I'll ask you one more time," Silas said, his words sharp and clipped. "Step aside, or I swear by the Great Master and all that you hold holy, I will ruin you!"

"I have an army at my disposal, boy," Deacon spat, taking another step toward us, eyes wild. "You can put the gun down, and walk away, in which case the Elders will decide your fate. Or you can stay with this worthless shell of a girl, and I'll have you watch while she is paraded in front of the entire commune, whipped, stripped, humiliated, and sent to the labor camp to die. Then you'll burn. I've done it before, Silas, I did it to your uncle, too! Choose, Silas. Which will it be?"

The expression on Silas's face never changed, and he never took his eyes off Deacon. "Suzannah, I'm sorry," he said.

He's turning me over to Deacon? My mouth fell open in surprise. Everything started moving in slow motion.

A sudden flash of light and a violent blast of sound erupted from the tip of the barrel of Silas's gun. Deacon stood with a look of complete shock on his face. A gaping hole in his chest was gushing blood. He raised his hand to his chest, thick red blood flowing over his fingers, dripping onto the floor. The shears fell from his hand and bounced across the tiles with a loud clang. The cockroaches skittered away.

"How?" he croaked.

He took a step forward, his mouth open in shock, then toppled forward, knocking me over.

Time rushed to catch up. I screamed and shoved Deacon's body off me. Silas grabbed my arms and pulled me to my feet.

"Silas, what have you done?" I sobbed uncontrollably.

"What I had to," he answered. I suddenly saw Silas in a different light. He was no longer a boy. He was a man, full-grown; strong, implacable, dangerous.

"We need to leave, now. There will be plenty of time for crying later when we're safe. Come on." He pulled me out of the room, not bothering to shut the door behind us.

I had no idea what Silas was planning to do. There was no escaping from Home. We had the tracking chip implanted in our wrists. They could find us, where ever we went. We would never make it past the graveyard before we were gunned down. The thought seemed somehow funny to me. At least we won't have far to go once we're dead. Death trying to escape seemed a better option than staying here and suffering execution and humiliation.

At this hour, everyone was already in their quarters, preparing for bed. Mercifully, no one appeared to have heard the explosion. One small blessing of being so far on the outskirts, I mused.

Silas led us into the woods that lined the perimeter of the commune, where we were hidden by the shadows before allowing us time to stop and catch our breath. He handed me his canteen, with the admonition to drink slowly.

I ignored him and guzzled the cool liquid, and nearly threw up when it hit my stomach.

He took a moment to caress my cheek, then a hard look crossed his eyes. I bowed my head, shamed at the realization of what he was seeing, a broken, disgraced girl. I expected him to hit me. Instead, he said, "I should have killed him long ago, and this wouldn't have happened to you. Forgive me, Suzannah."

I was stunned. I had brought him nothing but shame, and he was asking for my forgiveness? What kind of man was this?

I had no time for answers or further questions. Silas retrieved his canteen, then started us moving again. We stuck to the shadows, avoided militia patrols and finally arrived at his quarters.

Silas slammed the door open, sparking a surprised cry from Goody Maars.

"Mother, Papa," Silas said as the door banged against the wall so hard the doorknob left a mark on the wall.

"We're leaving the commune."

"Oh, Merciful Stars!" Goody cried, seeing us covered in blood. "Silas! Are you alright? Are you bleeding? What happened? Suzannah?"

"What have you done?" Dr. Maars asked, staring at us like he had never seen us before.

"Deacon's dead," Silas said. "I killed him."

"Heavens," Goody whispered, horrified.

"I knew this day would come. I hoped I wouldn't be alive to see it," Dr. Maars said. "We don't have much time. Marissa, get the children."

Dr. Maars grabbed me by my wrist and whipped out a blade from the table. "I'm sorry, Suzannah," he said, "but there is simply no time to do this any other way." He slashed at the back of my wrist and pulled out the tracking chip, letting it fall to the floor, the little light glowing green as it bounced. Goody Maars was already working on hers, tears running down her cheeks, her face white, before it finally flicked across the room. Then she started on Silas.

"Children, be strong," Goody Maars said, taking her daughter's wrist. Dr. Maars took Noah's wrist, and they started digging out the chips. Both children burst into tears at the pain but stifled their cries. I tied a boiled rag around my wrist to stem the flow of blood, then repeated the process for Telly and Noah while Goody sliced the microchip out of Dr. Maars' wrist.

"Papa, what's happening?" Noah asked. He looked scared. Telly just looked confused.

We rushed out of the room towards the stairs as fast as we dared. Dr. Maars fumbled for the elevator key, dropping it twice before he could turn the lock. Telly was sobbing.

"Shh," I shushed her.

She gulped back a sob. "I'm scared!"

"I know," I whispered as the elevator doors opened. "Me too."

The tension in the elevator was palpable. The doors shut and it went silent and dark, the only sound was the creaks and moaned of the elevator as it lowered itself, the raggedness of our breath and Telly's quiet sobs. I felt a hand grasp my own - it felt familiar; Silas.

He was with me. The people I loved most in the whole world were with me. This was my family. They'd die with me; there was comfort in that. I didn't think about what might happen should we survive. I had only room for only one thought - to get out of Home.

The bell dinged and the doors split open, startling my eyes with the dim light of the basement. We set out at a slow run, Silas pulling me along with his free arm and me holding Telly. I tried to slow down, the lack of food and the abuse of the past few days was taking their toll on my body, but Silas wouldn't let me fall behind. When we got outside, it was raining, turning the dirt into thick, sticky mud. We slogged through it, through the graveyard and into the woods.

Dr. Maars stopped when the alarm went off and the lights behind us started flashing red.

"Damn it," muttered Dr. Maars. It was the first time I ever heard him curse.

"Ephraim, what's wrong?" Goody asked.

He punching a button on some type of device and becoming more frustrated each time he pressed it. "Damn it," he said again, glaring into the tree line. "The bomb. The distraction bomb. It isn't working."

"What?" Silas cried. "All those nitroglycerin packets, all those years…"

"We must have wired something wrong," Dr. Maars

said. He was interrupted by the bay of hounds barking. Someone must have found Deacon's body. The militia was after us.

"Or something got in the way," Dr. Maars added." It doesn't much matter now. Come on. We're losing time. They're looking for us."

We ran along the trail until we heard the humming of Carriage House. "Silas," Dr. Maars shouted, "take these." He hefted the duffel bag full of books to his son. "And this." He shoved something into Silas's hands. "Take the car."

"Papa, no," he protested.

"Do it, son. Your mother and I will blow up the Carriage House."

"I can't do this without you. You have to come with us…" Silas began.

"Silas, I don't have time to argue. Take the children and go. Go to the Ruins. From there follow the highway north, Interstate 65. Keep going until you reach the border. Tell the Americans you're seeking asylum."

"I can't!" Silas shouted, his voice breaking.

"You can!" Goody said. "You must!"

"We'll wait for you at the Doctor's House," Silas shouted.

He gave me the bag and took my hand.

"Don't wait!" Goody Maars shouted after us. "We'll try to catch up, but if we don't you have to get the children to safety. Always remember that we love you! All four of you!"

I burst into tears. How could I leave this place without them?

I saw the tree: *Second star to the right, and straight on 'til morning...*

"Mama?" Telly cried as we dragged her away. "Mommy!"

My empty stomach lurched.

Silas led us through the woods, and I saw the split in the trail. *Two roads diverged in a wood, and I, I took the one less traveled by. And that has made all the difference...*

The hounds howled in the distance; I could faintly hear the sound of a man shouting commands. I carried Telly and followed Noah and Silas down the short path.

"Mama," Telly moaned into my ear. "I want my Mama!"

"So do I, Telly," I whispered as I ran. "So do I."

An explosion behind us shook the ground under our feet. Light bloomed. My ears rang from the deafening crack.

"They did it," Silas muttered. We stopped for a moment to see the fireball rise into the sky.

"Could they possibly have survived that?" I said.

"I don't know," Silas answered.

My legs suddenly felt weak. I almost dropping Telly.

"Come on," Silas said, but I noticed something new. I stood still and looked back at the commune. The sirens were no longer wailing. There were no lights from the search towers. Home was dark. Their power was gone.

Silas and coaxed us on down the trail.

The woods are lovely, dark and deep, but I have promises to keep, and miles to go before I sleep, and miles to go before I sleep...

At last, we came upon the Doctor's House. Silas pulled the car remote out of his pocket and stared at it as if looking for an answer to a question he didn't want to ask.

"We're waiting," he muttered.

"We have promises to keep," I whispered in agreement.

Goody promised to take me away with her family. I couldn't leave without her. We would wait for them, even if the militia found us.

Silas pulled the net off the hovercar and we stowed our things into the back storage area. I shoved the bag of books under the front seat.

"Take Noah and Telly, go into the house and hide," he ordered me. He placed something cold, heavy, and smooth into my hand. It was a small handgun. I had never held a gun before. I don't think any woman in Home had ever held a gun. I had no idea what to do with it.

"If anybody comes near you, pull this hammer back," Silas demonstrated the procedure, "point at their feet, and pull the trigger. Got it?" I swallowed and nodded. "The safety's off. I'll keep watch until Mother and Papa get here." He slung the rifle back over his shoulder. "I'll be in the trees." He grabbed me and kissed me, urgently, passionately. "Suzannah, I love you."

I didn't have time to process the kiss: it surprised me. The doorframe to the house was rotted, the door hung crooked. Silas kicked the door open, then ran into the trees. I watched him disappear into a large pine tree, then hustled the children inside the house.

The place smelled of old rotting wood and mildew. Discarded items from bygone years littered the floor. I took Noah and Telly and searched through the rooms, hoping to find an empty closet. I finally found one with that closet that would fit us all, then I dragged Noah and Telly in behind me and shut the door.

I could hear the rain dripping through the broken window, pattering down on the dilapidated roof. Telly sob quietly. I put my hand over her mouth to quiet her. She bit the palm of my hand so hard, I almost cried out. I couldn't see Noah, but I reached for him. He was wet, shivering, and shaking in the corner.

Then I heard something else; the sounds of soldiers and the hounds bawling into the night.

"What the hell is that?" a gruff voice asked.

"Just an old shack. Probably been here since before the war," someone else replied. "Think they might be in there?"

"One way to find out," the first voice said.

A dog barked, then the rest of the dogs joined in. A loud crack told me the front door had just been kicked in. They were in the house.

"Come on out, little whore," a soldier called. There were chuckles and the sound of breaking glass.

"Let's see if we can scare 'em out." A blast of gunshots burst and I screamed. I felt Telly go rigid in my arms. Noah didn't move, but I pulled him close.

"Did you hear that?"

The door to our room was kicked open. I held Telly as tightly as I could. "Don't make a sound," I whispered into her ear.

She stopped wiggling and went completely tense and rigid. I felt something warm on my leg; she was wetting herself.

Why hasn't Silas already killed them? I could hear them rummaging around in the room. It was only a matter of time before they opened the closet door. From the sounds of it, there were two soldiers and three hounds. Heavens, they had called the hounds on us? Of course. Why wouldn't they?

There was no way out. I had tucked the gun into the back of my skirt's waist and pushed the children into the corner, out of sight. The closet door flew open.

"Well, well, well. There she is. Come on out. You first, Suzannah."

I stood up, with the rifle in my face and the hounds barking.

"That's it. Come on. Now take your clothes off," one of the soldiers said in a frighteningly calm voice.

I shook my head and they laughed. But I was not going to submit to this again. I slipped my hands behind my back as if I were untying my skirt.

"That's a good girl," one soldier coaxed me as if I were a dog. My hands touched the cold steel of the gun. I gripped it with one hand, wrapping my fingers around the handle, settling my finger on the trigger, like Silas showed me. I took a deep breath, and I whipped it out.

My action was met with laughter.

I pulled back the hammer and they chuckled like I was a small child performing a cute trick. Heart thundering in my ears, I remembered Silas's instructions. I lowered the gun pointing it down at their feet. They assumed I was backing down, giving up, a cowering girl from the commune.

"That's it. Just put the gun down," he smiled at me, "then we can have a little fun."

I pulled the trigger, and the smile left his face.

There was a loud explosion of light and sound, and the soldier with the smile was splayed out on the floor. Screaming in pain. His companion was so surprised he dropped his rifle, and the dogs yelped and ran out of the room. I raised my gun and pointed it straight at him. I saw fear in his eyes, and I suddenly lost track of who I was. I wanted to make him hurt as much as I had been hurt. I pulled the trigger again, and his face disappeared.

The first soldier I shot wasn't dead yet. The bullet took him in the chest. He pressed a hand to his wound, swayed for a moment then saw his rifle, laying just out of his reach.

"You little bitch," he croaked. I pulled the hammer back as he struggled to reach his weapon.

His eyes glazed over and he fell back.

I had done this. I had taken down two soldiers. How?

A single thought raced through my mind: I have to find Silas and we have to get out of here.

I didn't know if the Doctor and Goody were still alive. I only knew they were not here yet. I hurried back to the closet and pulled Telly and Noah out, shoving the hot gun into the back of my skirt again, singeing my skin in the process. I had been burned much worse in the laundry.

Before I could get the children out of the house, I heard another group of militia approaching. They were apparently unaware of the altercation that had just taken place, for their taunts were filled with raucous laughter.

"Silas, you faggot, stop hiding!" someone shouted.

"Where is your whore?" another called out. "You know it's not polite to hoard a whore. We're all going to take a piece of her!"

"Yeah, share and share alike!" yet another laughed.

I looked out one of the broken-out windows to see if I could determine their direction of approach. I didn't see the militia boys, but to my amazement, I saw the Doctor and Goody running into the clearing together.

My joy turned to horror when Goody collapsed to the ground and cried out in pain.

"Marissa!" Dr. Maars shouted. He knelt beside her, trying to lift her up.

"Ephraim, go," Goody croak. "There's no way I'm making it there."

"I'm not leaving you," Dr. Maars declared through clenched teeth. He scooped his wife up and struggled to stand with her in his arms. "I'll never leave you."

A hand grabbed my shoulder. I spun, ready to pull the gun from my waistband, but it was Silas.

"Come on…" he started, but before he could finish his sentence, a group of soldiers sauntered into the clearing as if they were on a weekend hunting trip. They pointed their guns pointed directly at the couple.

"Don't make a sound," Silas hissed into my ear. "Get the children back in the room you were in. I'll be back for you in a moment." He elbowed a cracked window pane surrounding the door and slid the barrel of his gun through it. I didn't stay to watch. Whatever was about to happen, I knew it would involve bloodshed and much loss of life. Whether ours or theirs was the only variable.

I could hear course laughter from outside the house, dogs baying, and Goody crying in pain.

"Zeke, don't do this," Dr. Maars begged. Goody Maars sobbed as the soldiers laughed and mocked them both. "Stop, please! Zeke, don't you remember the nights you spent in our quarters? You were best friends with Silas and…"

"Shut up, old man," the soldier named 'Zeke' shouted. There was a thump and Dr. Maars cried out in pain. "Don't say my name in the same breath as that traitor. Watch and learn what happens to murderers. We're gonna take turns on your wife."

I squeezed my eyes shut, imagining that they were doing to her what was done to me yesterday. *No, not her, please, I thought. Please, God, get us out of here!* I squeezed Telly and Noah to me.

"And when we've finished with her, you can watch as we start on your daughter," Zeke added. "She'll be the youngest whore to ever join the Hard Labor camp." His fellow soldiers laughed as if that was the funniest joke they had ever heard, and urged him on.

There was a dull thunk, then another.

Suddenly the laughter stopped.

"What the hell? Zeke?"

There was a crash of what sounded like the front door being thrown open. I pushed the children behind me, then pulled the gun from my waistband and trained it on the door. If a soldier came through that door, he would die.

Instead, I heard Goody croak, "Silas?"

There was that thunking sound again, followed by a long silence, then a soft pow sound and someone cried out, "My knee."

I heard Silas say, "Papa?"

"I got some of the buckshot in my back," Dr. Maars replied. "I'll be okay, don't worry about me. Marissa?"

I warned the children to stay put, then made my way into the main room. Silas strode out into the clearing like the personification of death. Five bodies of young men who had once been his friends littered the ground. Silas marched over to the one soldier who was wailing and grasping his knee.

The soldier stopped wailing and started whimpering when Silas stood over him and placed the muzzle of his rifle against his temple.

"I don't blame you," Silas said in low, gravelly voice that sounded like it emanated from the pits of hell. "You're disgusting and selfish, but you're not an animal. Your great sin is believing what you've been taught.

"I let you live for a reason. I have a message for you to take to the people of Home. You tell them this: What the Elders are doing to the girls in the hard labor camps and the women in the commune is wrong. Perverting the Bible, desecrating it to perpetuate their own power, is sick. The Holy Book was never intended to be a weapon. It doesn't give the Elders or anyone else the permission to rape and defile and torture. You tell them, no woman ever deserves to be treated that way.

"Tell them: Come after us if you like. Retribution will be hell. Tell them this: Zeke, Horace, Thaddeus, Coltrane, Deacon - they are a fraction of the destruction they can expect. The graveyard in Home isn't big enough. Eye for an eye. Tooth for a tooth. Life for life. Mark my words."

Silas pulled his rifle away from the wounded soldier's head, knelt over him and looked him square in the face.

"You tell them."

The terrified soldier, looking more like a scared boy than a trained militia soldier, nodded.

Silas nodded, then did a quick search, relieving the soldier of his extra ammunition as well as his rations of food and water.

"But I need those..." the soldier whined.

"Tell it to the girls in the Hard Labor camp," Silas retorted.

Fear etched the soldier's face, as he struggled to stand. He hobbled off into the woods. Silas began searching the bodies of the dead, collecting their weapons and ammunition.

I went to the back room and gathered Telly and Noah into my arms, then brought them into the main room, where Dr. Maars was hunched over a limp form that resembled Goody Maars. Her clothes had been shredded; she was partially naked. I set the children down to go cover her, to pull her skirt back together, but Dr. Maars pushed me away. She wasn't moving.

"Is she dead?" I whispered.

"No. But she's been shot and she's bleeding out."

"I have to cover her," I sobbed.

"Why didn't you listen to me?" he shouted. I had never had Dr. Maars angry with me, and now he was yelling. "We told you to leave the moment you got to the car, not to wait!"

Goody's eyes fluttered open, and Dr. Maars let out a relieved breath.

"How bad?" she moaned.

"You're likely going to lose your leg."

"If that's what it takes," Goody croaked. "Twist it tighter."

Dr. Maars had wrapped a rag around her thigh and was twisting it with a stick. The flow of blood from her wound slowed then stopped.

Silas entered the clearing.

"Papa, we have to go."

Dr. Maars didn't look up. He continued working on Goody.

"Papa?" Silas repeated. "Ephraim!"

Dr. Maars looked up at Silas, surprised.

"We have to leave. Now. More are coming," Silas said.

Dr. Maars nodded. "Help me with your mother." he spoke softly to Goody, "Marissa, you have to hold the tourniquet in place."

"I'll try. Ephraim, it's all getting so hazy and..." she groaned as he picked her up. "Heavens!"

"Suzannah, get Telly and Noah," Silas instructed, although I was already picking her up.

Silas and Dr. Maars carried Goody to the hovercar and laid her across the back seat.

"Silas, hold the tourniquet in place, tight. Do not let it go or she will bleed out and die."

I struggled to carry the books, the weapons and the children to the car, but I had to set them down.

"Leave the guns," Dr. Maars said softly.

"We won't need them once we cross the border."

We all climbed into the hovercar, the children in the front seat with me and Dr. Maars at the controls, Silas in the backseat, looking down at the beautiful woman who had mothered me and loved me as if I were her own. She was covered in blood and dirt, leaves adorned her wet hair, her legs were exposed through her ragged skirt.

The wound on her thigh looked hideous, like a black crater, stark in the blue light that illuminated the inside of the car. She looked almost like a corpse, but she was still breathing. *She's still breathing!*

The hovercar lifted off the ground rose over the trees, and I felt that gentle thrust that said we were moving forward. A stray thought passed through my mind. *We're escaping from Home. We're safe.*

I felt light-headed. Black spots appeared before my eyes and started dancing, obscuring my vision. I realized I was exhausted. I was wet, chilled to the bone, and thirsty.

I looked out the window, back toward Home. I could see the emergency generator lights of the commune glowing faintly through the water droplets on the window. Specks of light, no doubt militia using lanterns, dotted the woods. *They can't touch us, now,* I thought. *We escaped.*

This place, this commune, was the only home I had ever known. It was no longer home to me. Had it ever been? What loomed ahead of us was darkness and trees and an uncertain future.

"Suzannah," Dr. Maars said in the kindly voice I had grown to love so much. "Look in the satchel. Is there a book still in there?"

I found the book bag, and I pulled out a leather-bound tome with faded gold lettering. The title read:

HOLY BIBLE

"Suzannah, start reading," Dr. Maars ordered his eyes on the road.

"Where?" I asked.

"Where else?" he replied. "At the beginning."

I flipped the book open and strained to see the words by the dim blue lights.

"In the beginning, God created the heavens and the earth. Now the earth was formless and empty, darkness was over the surface of the deep, and the Spirit of God was hovering over the waters.

And God said, "Let there be light," and there was light..."

EPILOGUE

My eyes cracked open to a bright, milky light. I blinked until my vision adjusted. I wasn't sure how long I had been asleep, but we were still flying over the interstate. Telly and Noah were huddled together, still asleep in front seat. The Bible had fallen to the floor panel. Dr. Maars still drove, grim determination lined his face. He looked years older than before.

I noticed my own reflection in the cracked side-view mirror. My face was covered in blood and dirt, leaves and pine needles in my hair. There was a stench of urine mingled with blood. I still ached in my private parts where I had been violated. *Will that pain ever go away?* I wondered.

I glanced over at Goody Maars and Silas. Silas was awake, still holding his mother's hand, still keeping pressure on the tourniquet on her leg. Goody was ashen, gray, like a statue with a disfigured face.

I looked away. There were too many emotions roiling inside me. I stared out the window upon an unfamiliar landscape. My eyes grew wide as I realized I was looking at row upon row of cultivated plants; not the stunted, meager crops of Home, but tall, green stalks, beautiful against the bluest sky I had ever seen.

In the midst of those fields were giant machines, like black and white metal spiders, plucking bits of plants and tossing them into container.

"What is that?" I whispered, pointing.

"That's a farm," Dr. Maars answered. "That machine is a pruner."

"Where are the workers?"

"The machine does the physical labor. It frees up the people to work in other areas."

"It's so big." I stared, overwhelmed at the enormity of what was below us. "How many people do you think it feeds?"

"Sixty thousand." Dr. Maars said. "Perhaps more."

"Sixty *thousand*?" I repeated, gawking.

"Children, you need to keep in mind that once we cross the border, we are refugees. We are not citizens. We have no rights there. We're at the American's mercy. I hope I've bought us enough sympathy over the years with all the secrets I fed them in the Ruins. I hope they'll take pity on us. I hope that they accept us as members of their society."

I thought about his words. Dr. Maars and Goody were trained physicians. Silas was a trained warrior. Telly and Noah were innocent children. They all had value. My own brokenness haunted me.

"I'm not worth anything anymore," I muttered.

"You are," Dr. Maars countered. He reached back to me and patted my knee.

I gasped and jerked away. I remembered! Morris did that before, groping me.

"I'm sorry," Dr. Maars apologized. "I forgot what you've been through. Please forgive me," he whispered.

I nodded, then glanced at Goody. I wasn't the only one who had suffered loss. "God forgive us all," I said.

Noah opened his eyes. "Where are we?" he said, stretching.

"Almost to the border," Dr. Maars said.

"Papa?" Silas said. "What about you?"

"Don't worry about me," Dr. Maars said.

A fence loomed in the distance. Two men in uniform stood at a station house beside a gate. Beyond the gate, the road was glowing like an illuminated river. And the words *Welcome to the United States of America: E Pluribus Unum* flowed across it.

"I've never seen anything like it," I breathed.

"I think we're going to see a whole lot of things we never imagined," Dr. Maars said. "Soon. Very soon."

ACKNOWLEDGEMENTS

First and foremost, I have to thank the all-holy Holy Trinity and the Life-Giving Theotokos for my getting published. I know it was not just hard work, it was a lot of prayer that got me this far.

Secondly, I have to thank Mike and Paula Parker at WordCrafts Press for taking a chance on an unknown writer who was struggling to get past the "I'd like to see more" response phase from literary agents.

I like to think that part of the reason HOME came to me like it did was because Bryan Sunday-Booth (may his memory be eternal) saw me struggling in his peripheral focus… while he was dying. Bryan reached out and helped me in a way I wasn't able to return. Namaste, Bryan.

Thank you to my personal cheerleaders in this journey, Rachel P. Allen, Angela Gimlin, Dr. Elyce Helford, Nina Holloway, Kevin Kirkpatrick, Amanda Moores, Toni Morgan, Jess H. Townsend, and Amber Cason Wingfield. Also thank you to my ARC readers, Dorothy Dyer, Shala Haslam, Melanie McFarlane, Kim Maxwell, Margaret Szklany-Brown, Hattricia Johnson, Malinda Brafford, Samantha Sanders, Patti Long-Lee, Elias McClellan, Emma Hawkins, Janet Gimlin, Fulton

Fry, Jennifer Ondig, Sherry Sunday-Booth, Jill Williams, Amy Forrester, Becca Anderson, Wesley Rutledge, Laura Kreitzer, Elisa Dane, Toni "Joan of Dark" Carr, Martina McAtee, and Amber Kizer (sorry the ARC got to you so late! Eek!). Beyond that, I've got many other friends (I'm probably forgetting) who did some proof-reading, fact-finding, or just plain prayed for me, and for that, I'm sorry that I forgot you here in the acknowledgments section. I hope you accept my humblest apologies.

Thank you as well to Jennifer Rainey, MMFT, and the Refuge Center in Franklin, Tennessee. I hope your mission continues to grow and create new advances in psychology, and continues to save lives.

Also a big thank you to another place: the Delinquent Debutantes.

And finally, I'd love to tease my parents for being worried I'd never get a book in print. >_< But I'll refrain. *For now.* Thank you for instilling that love of reading and writing in me.

Thank you, Mema, for giving me my first typewriter, too. May your memory be eternal.

And my siblings who may have rolled their eyes a little bit when I said I wanted to be a writer, thanks for not teasing me about it.

I thank God for everyone I mentioned in these acknowledgments (even the people I missed that I am thankful to). It takes a village to raise a child, and you can see that my "child," **HOME** was raised by a whole lot of people just looking here in my acknowledgments.

ABOUT THE AUTHOR

Eleni McKnight is a graduate of the University of Tennessee's Bachelor of Arts program and a patron of the Arts in her native Murfreesboro, Tennessee.

HOME is her first novel.

Follow her online at: www.elenimcknight.net
Twitter: @eleniwriting
Facebook: www.facebook.com/eleni.mcknight/
Pinterest: www.pinterest.com/eleniwriting/

Also Available From:

WORDCRAFTS PRESS

When Kings Clash
    by J.E. Lowder
The Scavengers
    by Mike Parker

Odd Man Outlaw
    by K.M. Zahrt

Maggie's Refrain
    by Marcia Ware

The Awakening of Leeowyn Blake
    by Mary Parker

Obedience
    by Michael Potts

www.wordcrafts.net